Also by Craig Robinson, Adam Mansbach, and Keith Knight

Jake the Fake Keeps It Real

JAKE THE FAKE

GOES FOR LAUGHS

CRAIG ROBINSON   ADAM MANSBACH
ART BY KEITH KNIGHT

CROWN BOOKS
for YOUNG READERS
NEW YORK

Text copyright © 2019 by Craig Robinson and Adam Mansbach
Cover art and interior illustrations copyright © 2019 by Keith Knight

All rights reserved. Published in the United States by Crown Books for Young Readers, an imprint of Random House Children's Books, a division of Penguin Random House LLC, New York.

Crown and the colophon are registered trademarks of Penguin Random House LLC.

Visit us on the Web! rhcbooks.com

Educators and librarians, for a variety of teaching tools, visit us at RHTeachersLibrarians.com

Library of Congress Cataloging-in-Publication Data is available upon request.
ISBN 978-0-553-52355-3 (trade) — ISBN 978-0-553-52356-0 (lib. bdg.)
ISBN 978-0-553-52357-7 (ebook)

Printed in the United States of America
10 9 8 7 6 5 4 3 2 1
First Edition

This book is dedicated to my family, who
keeps me strong; my fans, who continue to lift me up;
my incredibly talented nieces and nephews, who will
soon capture your hearts; and all the readers, who
disappear deeper and deeper into the world they are
discovering with every page they turn.

—C.R.

For Zanthe

—A.M.

To my little nephew, R.J.!
Read on, neff! Read on!

—K.K.

Before the show begins...
Please make sure all cell
phones are left **ON**, turned up
& set on the most *obnoxious*
ringtone ever!!

CHAPTER 1

It's a good thing that the end-of-semester talent show at Music and Art Academy is followed by the end of the semester. First there was the stress of wondering how I was going to pull off playing the only song I could really play on the piano without being discovered as the fake I was. Then came the excitement of spontaneously figuring out onstage that, while I was a fake as a musician, I was actually a natural at comedy.

I needed a break.

CRACK ← NOT THAT KIND OF BREAK!!

A chance to reevaluate my life, preferably while lying on a beach and drinking something with a miniature umbrella sticking out of it.

They ran out of tiny umbrellas

I got my wish in the form of a one-week family vacation to the Florida Keys.

Although it wasn't quite as relaxing as I would have liked because:

a) Florida is one of the weirdest places in the world. It's basically a swamp, but people decided to live there anyway, even though there are insects the size of Volkswagen Beetles and some of them have been elected to public office.

Also, the hot swampy weather seems to make people go bat-guano insane and do really deranged things. I even found a website devoted to this phenomenon, called FloridaOrGermany.com, where they tell you about all these nutty and super-disturbing news items and you have to guess whether they happened in Florida or Germany. Like, "man running across freeway holding bucket of worms attacked by man running across freeway holding bucket of fishing rods" or "city water commissioner found guilty of pooping in reservoir."

I got pretty good at guessing, actually. As a general rule, the ones that seem like they're probably caused by extreme sunstroke are Florida, and the ones that are so creepy they're beyond anything sunstroke could ever make you do are Germany.

b) Reading up on all the Florida weirdness made me jumpy and suspicious, so that even when we were just sitting at a restaurant or lying on the beach, I kept looking at everybody—the waiter, the guys riding on super-loud WaveRunners, the other vacationing families—and expecting them to start acting like lunatics. Which never actually happened.

Speaks only in KLINGON SLANG

Bathes exclusively in fermented mushroom gravy

I did get to swim a lot and eat some excellent seafood, including lots of local dolphin, which is a fish, not a smarter-than-us, able-to-read-at-an-eighth-grade-level mammal, and if you are asking yourself why Floridians have chosen to name their sandwich fish the same name as the most beloved aquatic creature of all time, then you have not been paying attention to what I've been saying about Florida.

TYPICAL FLORIDA MEAL:

KEY LIME PIE

Alligator bites!!

Hola, !⊙☆!!

CUBAN SANDWICH

Wears 9 pairs of undies at same time

Thinks he's Napoleon

I'm actually surprised they didn't also have a dish called human eyeballs that is actually a green salad, or a dish called mountain of puke that is actually french fries.

Human eyeball salad is rich in Vitamin "see"!!

But the main thing that prevented Florida from being relaxing was:

c) my big sister Lisa's decision, on the first day of the trip, to tell my parents that her thoughts about college were "evolving."

Lisa is a senior at Music and Art Academy, but not *just* a senior. She is more like a magical creature who floats on a cloud of pixie dust and barfs cotton candy and pees sparkling streams of delicious strawberry elixir.

She would be voted Most Likely to Succeed if M&AA did stuff like vote people most likely to succeed. Lisa can sing better than anybody you are likely to hear on the radio, and she is one of those people who, if you saw her wearing a snot-covered raincoat and shoes on her hands, your first thought would be "Oh, I guess snot-covered raincoats and shoes on your hands must be in fashion now." Plus, she is generally good-natured and never intentionally lords her perfection over anybody, even me. But it is still mega-annoying, since if there is anything I'm not, it's a perfect unicorn-like being who is good at everything. I'm more like the unicorn's comic-relief sidekick, Stinky the Pig.

Naturally, Lisa got a full scholarship to the college of her choice. In fact, colleges she hadn't even applied to sent her admission letters and boxes full of cash and puppies.

Red Sox gear!!

Lobster!!

Puppies!!

A Prince Impersonator!! HARVARD

YALE

STUFF COLLEGES HAVE SENT TO LISA

A dartboard!

Mew!!

Kitties

Princeton

Dartmouth

A 4-year pass to Google's campus cafeteria!!

google

Stanford

MON RIGHT THE PHI DOLPHIN

Berkeley

Not really. But you get the idea.

So there we were, me and my parents and Lisa, chillaxing on a serene beach and staring out at water so blue it was almost fluorescent, and out of nowhere

Lisa opened her mouth and said, "I've been thinking. College will always be there. But it just kind of feels like now is the time to really go for it, as far as making the whole band thing work. So I think I'm gonna defer my acceptance for a year."

I wasn't even a part of this discussion, and I could feel my throat closing up like I'd been poisoned. There was a pause approximately as long as the Ice Age and twice as cold, and then my dad said, in a very slow and fake-patient voice, "What band, Lisa?"

She took off her sunglasses and scrunched up her eyebrows at him, like she couldn't believe he'd ask her something so insulting. Which wasn't really fair, since as far as I knew, the band she was talking about was only a couple of weeks old, and I only knew about it because they practiced in our basement, which meant I couldn't play video games there.

"My conceptual art band, Daddy," Lisa said.

"I was not aware that you had a conceptual art band," my mother said in a voice you could scrape frost off.

CONCEPTUAL ART BAND
AT PRACTICE

Lisa nodded enthusiastically. Either she didn't notice Mom's tone or, more likely, she was doing a brilliant pretending-not-to-notice-Mom's-tone impression.

"Totally," she said. "It's called Conceptual Art Band."

"How conceptual," my dad said.

"Right?" said Lisa, like she was pumped that he got it. "It's me and Pierre."

Pierre is Lisa's boyfriend of the past two years. He's also a senior at M&AA, where he mostly paints gigantic mauve canvases that I don't personally like but other people seem very enthusiastic about.

Before that, he was into ceramics, and before that, beatboxing, tap dancing, miming, tuba, and ceramics again. Lately, he's been talking about taking up interpretive water ballet. But apparently Conceptual Art Band was the biggest deal of all.

"Pierre and me," my mother corrected Lisa, which seemed a little beside the point to me, but I busted in with a joke anyway.

"You're in the band, too, Mom?"

That got me a look of *Butt out, Jake.* So I did.

"Why can't you go to college *and* be in a band?" my dad asked. "I'm pretty sure it's been done before. Maybe you've even heard the expression 'college band.'" My dad tends to get sarcastic when he's stressed.

"I know," said Lisa. "But that's just it. We're not a college band. We're a conceptual art band. And if I'm going to make it work, I need to focus. College would be a distraction."

That left my parents pretty much speechless.

"Just for a year," Lisa said in what I guess was supposed to be a reassuring voice. "I'll still go to college. Unless Conceptual Art Band gets huge."

ART BAND GETS HUGE!

Maybe I should've stayed in college...

Zzz...

"We'll talk about this later," my mom said in a voice that sounded like it had been clipped by garden shears. But she and my dad both know that when Lisa sets her mind to something, she's like a pit bull clamping its jaws around a bone—she doesn't let go or get distracted, and you can't convince her to give it up. But those were the exact qualities that had made her so successful and perfect up until now, and I knew my parents weren't sure what to do, because as much as they wanted their kid to go to college, just like all parents want all kids to go to college, they also knew that letting Lisa do what Lisa was passionate about had pretty much worked out so far. Plus, maybe they weren't sure they could force her to go to college even if they tried.

The only good thing about Lisa's announcement was that it took the attention off me and my new thing of doing comedy, which I was getting kind of nervous about. On one hand, it was exciting to have found something I seemed to be good at and maybe even enjoyed. On the other, I didn't have any idea what to do next. I'd just opened my mouth and jokes had come out, but I couldn't keep doing that indefinitely.

I had to figure out what comedy really was and stuff, like when Luke Skywalker goes to the remote system of Dagobah to learn the ways of the Force from the ancient Jedi Master Yoda or whatever.

I worried about it for a couple of days, while Mom and Dad and Lisa discussed college and dreams and responsibilities and it became clear that Mom and Dad were not going to win. Then I decided to stop turning a good thing into a bad thing and put it out of my mind until I was back in school. After all, this was vacation. So instead, I worried about whether to go parasailing with Lisa, and specifically whether I might fall out of the harness and break my legs hitting the water and then get ripped apart by sharks. None of which ended up happening. Hooray.

CHAPTER 2

"I never thought I'd be excited to go back to school," I told my best friend, Evan. It was Sunday night, and I'd just returned from Florida, and we were in my basement, playing a new game we'd invented. It was called sockball, and the goal was to throw a balled-up pair of socks across the room and hit the other person. Five points for the head, three for the chest, one for arms and legs. You weren't allowed to move out of the way.

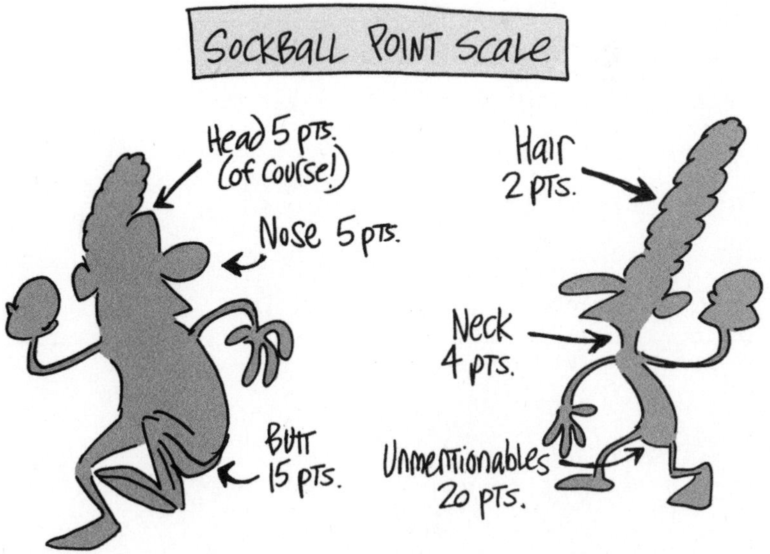

SOCKBALL POINT SCALE

Head 5 pts. (of course!)

Nose 5 pts.

Butt 15 pts.

Hair 2 pts.

Neck 4 pts.

Unmentionables 20 pts.

It was strangely relaxing, and you could talk while you played. The score was 243 to 211. I was getting creamed, which is what usually happened when I played anything with Evan.

"Right," said Evan, whipping the sockball and hitting me square in the nose. "Because you're a star now."

"I'm not a star." I threw the sockball back, aiming for the head and grazing Evan's shoulder. "I'm lucky I didn't totally bomb and get kicked out. But even doing one of Mr. Allen's crazy assignments is better than listening to Lisa and my parents have the same argument for seven straight days."

Evan threw, and the sockball bopped me in the neck.

"What's neck?" he asked.

"How about four?"

"Okay."

"That reminds me," I said. "Lisa and Pierre want us to be in some video after school tomorrow. For a song called 'The Ballad of the Duck-Billed Platypus.'"

Evan shrugged. "I got nothing better to do." Then he pegged me right in the face.

● ● ●

Usually I take the bus to school because I have to be there at eight a.m. sharp, whereas Lisa gets picked up by Pierre at like ten-thirty because seniors can make their own schedules and avoid early classes. But since it was the first day of the semester, we all had to show up early. So I snagged a ride.

Pierre's car is like the universe before the Big Bang, when all the matter in existence was crammed into one tiny, super-dense dot. Or, in this case, one medium-size van.

"What's up, Obi-Wan Ken-bro-be?" he said as he opened the passenger door for Lisa like some chivalrous knight of the Middle Ages, except that when he did it a soda can and two chicken bones fell out onto the street, and Lisa had to pick them up daintily with two fingers and toss them back into the car.

OTHER CHIVALROUS KNIGHTS!!

GLADYS

Michael

Don't hassle The Hoff!! (ask a parent)

Keith

I drew this book just for YOU!!

"Not much, Shoeless Bro Jackson," I said, clambering into the backseat. I pushed aside a rubber chicken, a paint-encrusted paintbrush, and a giant, almost-empty movie theater popcorn tub, and put on my seat belt.

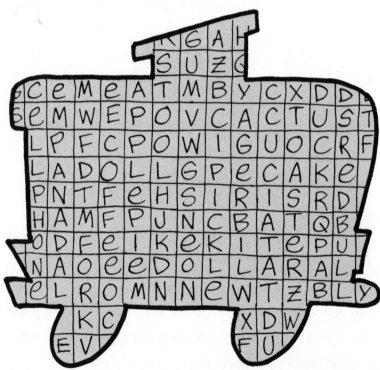

CAN YOU FIND ALL THE STUFF IN PIERRE'S VAN?

"I ran into Mr. Allen over the break," Pierre said as we cruised down the block. "He's psyched about your comedy thing, little dude."

"He said that?"

"Uh-huh. I was at a yard sale, looking for costume stuff for the video, and there he was, going through old record albums.

"He pulled out a bunch of comedy ones, like old Steve Martin stuff, and said he was gonna tape them for you."

I started to get a sinking feeling in my stomach, like I had swallowed a ten-pound barbell. The last thing I needed was the added pressure of Mr. Allen deciding to get personally involved in my "career."

Without thinking, I reached into the tub of popcorn and grabbed a handful and shoved it into my mouth.

It tasted like it was six months old. I spat it back into the tub.

"Tape them?" I said. "Why, were the covers splitting apart or something?"

Then it hit me: he meant "tape" as in record onto cassette tape. That was Mr. Allen for you: buying music on one obsolete medium and transferring it to another obsolete medium. Where was I going to get a cassette player? An old folks' home?

Lisa turned around and smiled at me. "Sounds like he's expecting big things, inorganic compound Chromium Bro-mide."

"With big expectations come big disappointments," I told her.

"Sounds like loser talk," Lisa replied.

"Yeah," I agreed. "It does, doesn't it?"

"Don't worry," Pierre said. "When Conceptual Art Band blows up, you can drop out of school and be our roadie. I mean, our bro-die."

I was opening my mouth to say a nice sarcastic *Thanks a lot, Bro-ce Springsteen,* but just then Pierre turned on the radio and some classical violin piece blared out of the speakers at a volume of 267, so I just shut up for the rest of the ride.

The first person I saw when I walked into school was my friend Azure, but it took me a second to realize it was her.

A normal outfit for Azure would be:

- a spiderweb drawn with eyeliner that covers half her face

- one pink glove with the fingers cut off
- a T-shirt for a punk band she stole from her dad
- a baby's shoe worn as a necklace
- a flannel shirt tied around her waist
- fake pearl earrings
- a pair of headphones connected to nothing

But not today.

I gave her a hug and said, "Why are you dressed like that?"

"Like what?"

"Like you're about to go play golf on a sailboat with people named Muffy and Chip," I said, tugging on the arm of the yellow sweater she had tied around her neck.

"Did you run out of eyeliner or something?"

Azure shrugged. "New semester, new look. Prep is the new punk, dude."

"So then what's the new prep?"

AZURE'S FASHION ~~HIS~~HERSTORY:

HER "BOX PERIOD"

HALF HORSE

BAWL-MOR STYLE!!

MS. P-NUT

LAST YEAR

THIS YEAR

MOON UNIT

PHRUIT PHASE

Azure thought for a second. "Hillbilly," she decided. "Come on, let's go to homeroom."

"We have, like, ten minutes before the bell."

"Early bird gets the worm!" she said, and grabbed my arm.

"Who *are* you? What worm?"

But Azure was already slamming open Mr. Allen's door. That's when I realized it wasn't just Azure who had changed over vacation. If not for the number on the door, I never would have believed this was my homeroom.

WRIGGLE WRIGGLE

BREAKFAST WITH AZURE

Just two weeks ago, it had been full of musical instruments—a piano, a drum set, even an accordion. All that was gone now. Instead, there was a terrarium that took up an entire wall, and a fish tank covering another. Giant tropical plants towered over everything, so thick you could barely see the ceiling, and it was super moist and hot, like somebody was breathing right in your face.

In the middle of the room was a microphone on a stand. Mr. Allen stood before it, wearing a safari jacket and a pith helmet.

"Testing," he said. "Four-five, four-five."

"Thank goodness," I said to Azure. "After our six-day trek through the rain forest, we finally found that comedy club everyone's been talking about."

Mr. Allen laughed into the mic. The mic responded with a jolt of earsplitting feedback. He stepped away from it and walked over to us. "Good one," he said. "Welcome back. I did some redecorating. What do you think?"

"Could use monkeys," Azure said thoughtfully. "Capuchins, maybe."

$$700 + 800X\left[56.09 - 176.6 + 32,000 \ \ 17,000 + (45,000 + 6500)\right.$$
$$+ 7000 + 70\left] - 4000 + 3 + 41,000 \ \ 76000 - 1 \ 0 < N\right.$$
$$\in X \, hp \ OCH * on = 86,000, 56,000 + 15,000 + 6500 \div (4,500,000)$$
$$+ 79,000 - 189) + 500 + 400 \ \ B \times D + 700 = (pop.\ py\ in\ 700)$$
$$E_2 + e \ CN\left(\frac{X^3}{X}\right)7 + \frac{N}{X}(1050X) \ \ 5,000,000 + -PN$$
$$\left[\frac{1}{3} + \frac{1}{4}X\frac{1}{2}2\right] = PN^2(X)\ net/s \ \ 600,000 - X_p \ X_r \ D_r =$$
$$cm \ \ 65,000 + 75,000 + 65,000. \ 1 \ pmX(1RW) - \frac{1}{2}) < kw$$
$$KP \ WP \ UP \frac{1}{65,000}X^2 + p^3 \times p^3 \frac{(VI\sqrt{6x-p})^2}{N \cdot 1} = capuchin \ monkeys!!$$

IT'S SO
obvious
WHEN you
WRITE IT
OUT!!

25

OTHER ODD CREATURES MR. ALLEN TRIED TO GET FOR THE CLASSROOM:

Mata-Mata Turtle

Madagascar Tree Frog

Cassowary

Okapi

Blobfish

Jaguar

Mr. Allen looked crestfallen. "I know," he said, shaking his head. "I tried. The school's insurance wouldn't cover it. "I got a snake, though. Check it out."

He led us over to the terrarium, and sure enough, a giant brown and green and yellow snake lay piled on top of itself beneath the bright lights. It was slithering very slowly, the folded coils of its body seeming to move in different directions as they slid past each other.

It was kind of hypnotic, and we all watched in silence for a few seconds. Then Azure whispered, "Guys, she's shedding!" I looked closer, and as the snake moved, she left behind a translucent snake-shaped skin, like an impossibly thin wrapper.

IMPOSSIBLY THIN WRAPPER

IMPOSSIBLY THIN RAPPER (SNOOP DOGG!!)

"Wow," I said. It was the most graceful thing I'd ever seen, and I am *so* not a snake person.

"That's what we're all doing," Mr. Allen murmured. "Shedding our old skins and growing new ones. Which reminds me—Jake, I have something for you." He straightened up and strode across the room.

I tore myself away from the terrarium. "Yeah, Pierre said he ran into you at a yard sale . . . ," I began, expecting him to take some cassettes out of his desk. If he still had a desk, anyway. I couldn't see one through all the mist in the air. Which I assumed was a combination of spray bottle water, because there were spray bottles everywhere, and the fact that the heat was cranked up to like ninety-five degrees.

But I was wrong. Mr. Allen came back with a slip of paper. He handed it to me with a big smile on his face and waited.

I opened it and read:

Mr. Allen was beaming at me like I'd just read the winning Powerball numbers. "Do you know who that is?" he asked.

"Some old guy?"

"Do you know *which* old guy?"

Mr. Allen's eyes shone with excitement, and sweat was beading on his upper lip. Though that was probably from the insane temperature of the room.

"There are so many of them," I said.

"Maury Kovalski is a comedy legend," Mr. Allen informed me. "One of the last real, old-school, dyed-in-the-wool Catskills stand-ups."

That meant absolutely nothing to me, but I nodded like it was totally awesome.

Why are dogs sniffin' butts all the time?

A YOUNG MAURY SLAYIN' IN THE CATSKILLS!!

"Totally awesome," I said.

"He's an old buddy of mine," Mr. Allen explained. "I told him I had an aspiring comedian in my class who could use some advice from a professional, maybe some help really discovering his voice, and he . . ." Mr. Allen trailed off.

"He what?"

"You should go see him," Mr. Allen said. "Just knock on his door. He's always home."

"He what?" I asked again. "You didn't finish your sentence."

"He's really nice once you get to know him," Mr. Allen said, and turned away to water his jungle.

CHAPTER 3

The next day after school, I went home and got my bike and rode it out to Willow Greens Retirement Home, which was only a few miles from my house. I don't know what I was expecting, maybe a big sprawling mansion like Professor Charles Xavier's pad in the X-Men movies. Or something on a golf course, like my grandpa Dan's place in North Carolina, where kids aren't allowed to spend more than two nights, which is a) bogus and insulting, but b) convenient, since two days there is about all I can take.

Willow Greens was more like a motel, with two floors and long outdoor hallways. A run-down motel, in the kind of neighborhood where you have to do your grocery shopping at the 7-Eleven. It definitely didn't seem like the kind of place a famous retired comedy genius would live, unless he had managed his money very, very badly.

I locked my bike up and took the front wheel with me just to be on the safe side.

Maury Kovalski's apartment was on the first floor. My heart was pounding in my chest as I knocked. It was kind of weird, just showing up like this. Then again, Mr. Allen hadn't steered me wrong so far.

After a moment, an old guy with a full head of white hair and bushy white eyebrows and three or four days' worth of white stubble on his cheeks answered the door. He

Guard dog

was wearing a bathrobe and eating yogurt out of an enormous tub with an enormous spoon.

He looked me up and down and said, "Wheel salesman, eh? No thanks, I just discovered fire yesterday. Come back in fifty to sixty thousand years."

He started to close the door, but I stuck my foot out and caught it.

"Wait, Mr. Kovalski. My name is Jake. Mr. Allen sent me."

"Oh, so you're his muscle, huh? Well, go ahead then, you goon, do your worst. I don't have the money."

VARIOUS GOONAGE SENT TO MAURY KOVALSKI'S DOOR

Mr. Kovalski's expression was so deadpan, I couldn't tell if he was joking. Then I remembered that a) he was a comedian, b) there was no such thing as a door-to-door wheel salesman, c) nobody hires a sixth grader as muscle, and d) Mr. Allen wouldn't send goons to his friend's house anyway.

Therefore, I concluded that e) this guy was freaking hilarious.

"Okay," I said, deciding to play along. "You asked for it, Kovalski. I'm gonna break both your legs. But don't worry, I brought a wheelchair. Compliments of Mr. Allen. Next time maybe you'll think twice before borrowing money for calf implants and not paying it back."

Mr. Kovalski eyed me for a few seconds, then shoved his gigantic tub o' yogurt at my chest.

This 'gurt's got more active cultures than the opening ceremony of the summer olympics!!

YOGURT

"Have some yogurt, kid."

"Uh, no thanks," I said.

"Well, don't just stand there. Come in. Or leave. Or just stand there. On second thought, that's fine, too."

I followed him inside. The room was messy, a combo kitchen/living room with an old TV in one corner and stacks of books and records covering half the couch.

Over the stove was a microwave oven with the door open. It was filled with books.

"So," I said as Mr. Kovalski sank down onto the couch, "you do a lot of cooking?"

"A wiseacre, eh?" was his reply.

I shrugged and put my hands in my pockets. "Better than a dumb-acre."

"Mmphh," Mr. Kovalski grumbled. "So you wanna be a comedian, huh?" He spread his arms. "Live in splendor, like me? What makes you think you're so darn funny, huh? What'd you do, make a fart joke, get a little laugh, decide this is the life for you?"

I didn't know how to answer that, so instead, I said, "Mr. Allen thought I could use some advice from a professional."

"You and me both, kid."

"He said you were a legend." I couldn't remember if he'd actually said that, but I figured a little flattery couldn't hurt.

"I hate that word. Sasquatch. The Abominable Snowman. The Loch Ness Monster. Those are legends. Me, I'm just an old forgotten stand-up eating yogurt out of a giant tub."

ABOMINABLE
SNOWMAN

KIDS!! PUT ON
your special
3-D glasses
for full effect!!

BIGFOOT

YOGURT

"It smells a little bit like Bigfoot in here, if that makes you feel better."

Mr. Kovalski snorted and sat up straighter. "First lesson of stand-up, kid. You ready? I don't see a pen in your hand."

"Should I look in the refrigerator for one?"

Normally I would never have been so rude to an

adult, much less one I'd just met, but somehow it seemed like the rules were different with Mr. Kovalski. We were speaking a different language. The language of comedy. Or of being a jerk. Maybe those were the same language, actually.

"Very funny. You listening, you schlemiel? This part is serious."

"What's a schlemiel?"

"It's a Yiddish word. The schlemiel is the guy who spills the soup. The schlimazel is the guy it lands on."

Mr. Kovalski shook his head. "This is comedy gold right here. You should be writing this down!"

"I have a good memory. What was the other thing?"

"What other thing?"

"The first lesson of stand-up. The thing you were going to tell me before you called me a schlemiel."

"Oh. Right. Here it is: always punch up, never punch down."

"That's it?"

"That's it."

"I don't get it."

"You will. Or you won't. What do I care? I got my yogurt."

"How about teaching me a joke or something?"

Mr. Kovalski shook his head. "No, no, no. You can't teach a joke. A comic has to *make* the joke. Like . . . a pot. Or . . . a cheese. As a matter of fact, lemme tell you a joke about that. There's this fella, right? Goes to prison."

"What for?"

"Doesn't matter what for. Tax evasion. Shut your piehole and let me tell the joke. So on the first day, he's sitting in the cafeteria, and all of a sudden this big burly guy stands up and yells, 'Fifty-seven!' And everybody in the room starts bellowing with laughter.

I mean, they're laughing for a solid minute. And when it finally dies down, the guy says, 'Fourteen!' and again, everybody is rolling in the aisles.

"So the new guy, he nudges the fella next to him and says, 'What gives? What's so funny?'

"The guy next to him says, 'Eh, we've all been here so long, we know all the jokes. So we just assigned them numbers, and now that's how we tell 'em.'

"Well, the new guy is very intrigued. And for the next three months, he studies all the jokes. Learns 'em backward and forward. And finally, he's ready. He stands up in the cafeteria, and he says, 'Hey, everybody! Twenty-nine!'

"Silence. Total silence. He can't understand it. He sits down, and he says to the guy next to him, 'What'd I do wrong?'

"The guy next to him shrugs and says, 'Some people just can't tell a joke.'"

Maury Kovalski leaned back on the couch, looking very satisfied with himself.

It was at that moment that I knew I was in the presence of a comedy genius. Either that, or a lunatic.

● ● ●

GENIUS   LUNATIC

CONSTANTLY
CARRIES A
TUB OF YOGURT
AROUND

WEARS BATHROBE
& BUNNY SLIPPERS
ALL DAY

DOES NOT
TRUST
JOGGERS

ONLY BATHES IN
ANTIBACTERIAL
FOAM

When I got back home, Evan and Lisa and Pierre and six or seven kids I knew and semi-knew and didn't know were waiting for me in the kitchen. All of them were angry. Some of them were eating guacamole. My dad makes excellent guacamole.

"What the heck, man?" Lisa said the second I walked in, my mind still reeling from the visit with famous comedy non-legend Maury Kovalski. "Did you forget?"

"Forget what?" I asked, which was basically a long way of saying yes. Then I noticed that Evan was wearing a giant and very realistic foam-and-rubber walking-egg costume. Maybe "realistic" is the wrong word, since there's no such thing as a walking egg. But if there was, it would have looked like Evan.

"The *video*, influential 1960s underground comic book artist Vaughn Bro-de," said Pierre while juggling three avocado pits.

"Now go put on your walking-egg costume," my

sister added. "Chop-chop. We only have the trampoline rented until six."

Five minutes later, Evan and I were bouncing up and down in our costumes—which were not easy to move in, although they were extremely easy to sweat in—while Pierre and Lisa lip-synched along to their own vocals and the rest of the cast executed a surprisingly complicated series of dance moves.

"The Ballad of the Duck-Billed Platypus" went like this:

Not quite a reptile, not quite a mammal
He's like Alan Trammel, but crossed with a camel
Not quite mammalian, but not quite reptilian
Partway a hero and partway a villain
He's stuck in between the one thing and the other
Not quite in uniform, not undercover
He lays eggs, he has fur, he's hard to describe
He's all of us, none of us—look in his eyes!
The duck . . . billed . . . platypus!
Don't . . . be . . . mad at us!
We must praise the D-Plat
In the key of B-flat
All niiiiiiight!

We did take after take, until my stomach and legs hurt from jumping. I frankly couldn't understand the song or the video concept, which, in addition to the walking eggs on the trampoline, involved a lot of dancing animals, vegetables, and I think minerals.

Between "The Ballad of the Duck-Billed Platypus" (which was not a ballad at all, incidentally, since a ballad is supposed to be slow and quiet, not fast and loud) and trying to make sense of my meeting with Maury Kovalski, I basically ended up overloading my brain, the result being that I passed out at seven-thirty p.m. like some type of five-year-old.

Also, in case you were wondering, Alan Trammel played shortstop for the Detroit Tigers in the 1980s. Pierre found that out when he was Googling "rhymes with mammal."

CHAPTER 4

On Tuesday, from deep inside his humid jungle lair, Mr. Allen gave us an assignment—the first one of the new semester. For a second, I was terrified: if our classroom was suddenly a rain forest and Azure was suddenly preppy, maybe Mr. Allen's assignments were suddenly going to make sense.

But my fear was unfounded. Mr. Allen wanted us to write a review of an "observed human activity" as if it was a piece of performance art.

Nobody knew what that meant. Klaus, the German exchange student who does not play drums for our no-instruments band Crazy American People Who Do Not Make Any

Assignment

Zense (which he also named), was the first to admit it.

"Zees assignment," he said. "Eez joke? Eef zo, Klaus doss not get."

Mr. Allen smiled without showing any teeth.

Klaus always plays when he's confused

"I get it," said my friend Forrest, who was home-schooled until this year and has some very strange ideas about the importance of squirrels in education, and also a slight fear of walls, ceilings, and floors. "We're supposed to learn about how nature is art. So we appreciate that no painting can ever match a sunset, and no sculpture can ever be as beautiful as a squirrel climbing an oak tree. Right?"

Mr. Allen shook his head. "No nature," he said. "Human activities only."

"Rats," muttered Forrest.

"Do you not lizzen?" Klaus asked him. "No rats. Rats are nature."

"It's an expression, Klaus," said Azure.

"'Rats' eez expression? Zees ees making no zense."

"You never think anything makes any zense," my friend Zenobia said. Then she thought about it for a second and added, "Maybe you're right."

"Okay then, so everybody gets it," Mr. Allen said. "Great."

About six kids raised their hands to indicate that they did not. I was one of them.

"Great," Mr. Allen said again. "Now. Let's check in with Hotch, shall we?"

Hotch is the snake. We all looked at each other and sighed sighs of *I guess we have to figure it out on our own.* We sigh those sighs a lot.

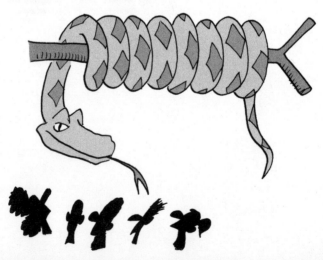

When I got home, I wandered from room to room, looking for a human activity to observe and write about. But nothing interesting was going on.

Nothing going on here... Just a sweaty Ham!!

I was hoping my parents and Lisa might be "discussing" college, meaning arguing about it, which is a frequent human activity in my house these days, but no such luck. My mother was doing her homework, which is what she calls it when she brings paperwork back from the office. Lisa and Pierre were huddled around the computer, editing video footage and eating a giant bowl of popcorn with brewer's yeast on it, which I'm convinced they put on there just to keep me away, the same way people put coyote pee on their plants to repel deer.

POPCORNOPALYPSE!!

The list of jobs I do not want, by the way, looks something like this:

1. Coyote pee collector
2. Guy who puts coyote pee in bottles
3. Coyote pee bottle inspector
4. Vice president of marketing for coyote pee company
5. Truck driver responsible for transportation of coyote pee
6. Farm employee in charge of spreading coyote pee on crops
7. Politician
8. Anything else involving coyote pee

Finally, I found my father in the kitchen, and inspiration struck.

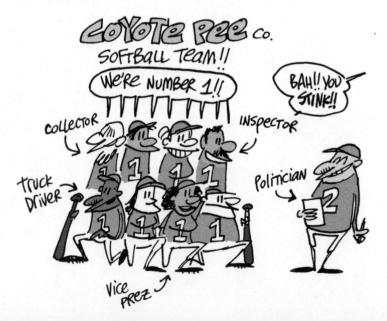

Clarence Frederick Liston Eats a Bowl of Cereal

A REVIEW BY JAKE LISTON

It was with great excitement that I found my seat for the much-anticipated show entitled *Clarence Frederick Liston Eats a Bowl of Cereal*, which premiered yesterday in the kitchen of Mr. Liston's comfortable but somewhat messy home. Fans of Mr. Liston's career may recall his previous groundbreaking works, including *Clarence Frederick Liston Eats a Turkey Leg* and *Clarence Frederick Liston Drinks a Glass of Milk*.

As the world's loudest chewer and swallower, Mr. Liston is one of the most dynamic live performers on the scene, able to create a symphony of sounds with nothing but his teeth and throat. It's as if he has an amplifier hidden inside his mouth. You could be anywhere in the house, and if he is consuming any type of food or beverage, you will know it. Even cheese, which you would think would be soundless. Even if you are watching TV. Or dead.

Last night's performance was an unusual one for several reasons. First of all, it is weird to eat a bowl of cereal at five-thirty p.m. Second, it is weird to eat a bowl of cereal less than an hour before you are about to eat a dinner of lasagna and salad—a dinner you yourself are about to start making. When asked about this by a member of the audience, Mr. Liston explained his philosophy that it is never a good idea to "cook on an empty stomach," and also that cereal is "delicious any time, not just for breakfast." He then proceeded to tell a story about how, in college, he often ate cereal "morning, noon, and night."

This story, which was at least an eight on the Boring Scale, delayed the performance by a full five minutes, causing Mr. Liston's audience to become somewhat fidgety.

Finally, it was the moment we had all been waiting for. Mr. Liston picked up his spoon, which was the largest spoon in the Liston household, not counting the giganto serving spoons, and dipped it into his bowl of Belchos, like an Olympic diver sliding into the water or a backhoe breaking ground.

The spoon emerged full of tan, perfectly round Cheerios, floating on a thin layer of nice white milk.

It is worth pointing out, for those unfamiliar with Mr. Liston's work, that he is a huge fan of milk, especially whole milk. In fact, he thinks other milks, such as two percent and nonfat, are "for the birds," though this is just an expression and Mr. Liston does not actually think that birds drink milk, as they are not even mammals.

The spoon hovered in midair, and the tension in the room was so thick you could cut it with a knife. What was Mr. Liston going to do? Would he put the spoon in his mouth? Would it fit? Would he miss his mouth and bang the spoon against his chin, spilling milk and tiny whole-grain morsels everywhere?

And then, with the grace of a ballerina standing on top of a tiger standing on top of a shark, Mr. Liston wrapped his lips around the spoon, and the milk and Cheerios disappeared into his mouth, and the spoon came back out empty.

The audience was on the edge of their seats, waiting for that first CRUNCH. And Mr. Liston did not disappoint. His teeth annihilated the cereal. It sounded like how you might imagine it would sound if a *Tyrannosaurus rex* bit into a school bus stuffed full of dried leaves.

The audience burst into applause, which seemed to surprise Mr. Liston for a moment. But then: He SWAL-LOWED. It was like the sound a four-ton boulder makes when you roll it off a hundred-foot-high cliff into a lake.

At this point the audience could not help leaping out of their seats in a standing ovation.

With an expertise that was awesome to behold, Mr. Liston then began to build up a steady rhythm of spoon dipping, mouth filling, cereal chomping, and swallowing.

If you closed your eyes and concentrated only on the sound, you might find yourself lulled and soothed by the regularity of it. But if you did this, you would miss out on all the visual parts of the drama, because as the performance went on, the issue of ingredient management began to emerge as a major theme in the work: Would Mr. Liston be able to balance the ratio of cereal to milk and finish big, with a final bite that left the bowl empty of both? Or would he miscalculate, and have to slurp up the extra milk?

But Mr. Liston is a professional, and the audience did not need to be concerned. His final bite cleared the bowl, and in an unexpected flourish, he stood up as he swallowed it (the final bite, not the bowl), treating the audience to the sight of his enormous Adam's apple bobbing down and then up again in his throat, and placed both his bowl and spoon in the sink.

All in all, it was an amazing show by an American genius at the top of his artistic game.

Mr. Liston will be offering repeat performances at seven-thirty a.m. every weekday for the foreseeable future. Seating is limited and on a first-come, first-served basis, and audience members are advised to bring earplugs.

CHAPTER 5

"You have to do it," Azure said to me in the cafeteria. Lunch that day was quinoa fritters with rémoulade, a grapefruit and lump crab salad, and carrot-ginger soup. It was delicious, but I could barely eat a bite. My stomach was all knotted up from the stress of everybody telling me what to do.

Lanyard Knot

Figure 8 Knot

Tom Fool Knot

Jake Stomach Knot!!

"You really should, dude," Zenobia agreed. "I'll come and watch."

"We all will," Azure added. "Even Mr. Allen, I bet."

"Zayink no iz not an opzhun!" Klaus shouted, slamming his fist against the table so hard all our plates rattled.

They were talking about open mic night at the Yuk-Yuk, which is a comedy club downtown. Every comedian who'd ever made anything of himself had performed there, according to Mr. Allen. Maury Kovalski himself had said the same thing, and also told me that the key to comedy was performing over and over and over again. Telling jokes to anyone who would listen.

To illustrate the point, he told me a story about Henny Youngman, a famous comedian from the dawn of time.

Henny had just come out of a comedy club and was walking down the street by himself, unaware that Maury had also come out of the club and was walking a few paces behind him. A pigeon was standing on the sidewalk, and Henny Youngman—who, as Maury made sure to point out repeatedly and loudly, THOUGHT HE WAS COMPLETELY ALONE—bent down and said to the pigeon, "Any mail for me?"

This was what made him a genius, Maury said. He told jokes even when there was no one there to laugh.

Just then, Forrest sat down across from me and dumped a giant bag of acorns onto the table. Nobody said a word. We all knew Forrest had trouble eating indoors. This was his way of coping.

HENNY YOUNGMAN (as depicted by Forrest)

Take my eggs, please!!

"So," he said, rolling an acorn between his palms, "you gonna do some comedy tonight or what?"

I took a deep breath and let it out slowly. "I guess it's what Henny Youngman would do, right?"

Forrest frowned. "How do you know my hen's name?" he asked.

"You have a hen?" said Zenobia.

"I have eighteen hens," Forrest replied. "My family likes eggs."

He was quiet for a moment, and then he looked up at me very seriously and nodded. "Yes," he said. "Yes, I think it is what Henny Youngman would do."

"Okay then," I said. "I guess I can't be a chicken, huh?"

Azure slapped her forehead. "You better be funnier than that tonight, dude."

"What, you don't like puns about poultry? You think they're fowl?"

Everybody groaned. I picked up my quinoa fritter, feeling suddenly hungry. Sometimes making a bad joke is way more satisfying than making a good one.

"So you'll perform?" Azure asked.

"Yeah," I said. "A stand-up has to stand up, I guess."

Azure leaped out of her seat. "I'm going to go make some posters!" she announced, and darted off.

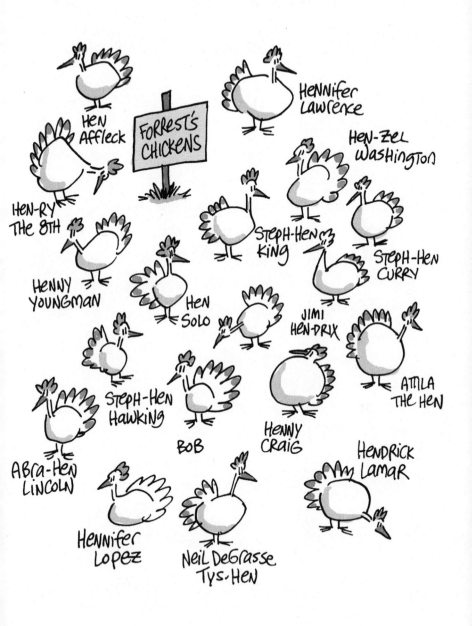

HEN Affleck

HENnifer Lawrence

HEN-ZEL Washington

HEN-RY The 8TH

FORREST'S CHICKENS

STEPH-HEN KING

STEPH-HEN CURRY

HENNY YOUNGMAN

HEN SOLO

JIMI HEN-DRIX

STEPH-HEN Hawking

BOB

HENNY CRAIG

ATTILA THE HEN

ABRA-HEN LINCOLN

HENDRICK LAMAR

Hennifer LOPEZ

Neil DeGrasse Tys-HEN

63

I stood up, too. "I guess I better go work on my set," I said.

The truth was, I'd been working on my set all week. Maybe all month. Ever since the talent show, I'd been writing down jokes. Except they weren't really jokes—not the kind with a setup and a punch line, anyway. They were more like observations about life, and weird ways of looking at things. I kept thinking back to the Music and Art Academy talent show. That day, I'd gotten laughs by making fun of the school—and that, if I understood right, was what Maury Kovalski meant by "punching up." You had to have targets that were bigger and more powerful than you.

Everybody wants to hear you diss the president. Nobody wants to hear you diss a baby.

Although, actually, I could see how dissing a baby might be kind of funny.

●●●

That night, the Yuk-Yuk was packed. My whole class showed up, just like Azure had promised. They were spread out over the front four tables—which obviously annoyed the heck out of the waitresses, since waitresses work for tips and my friends were ordering, like, one soda apiece and a side of fries to split six ways.

In the second row of tables were my parents, along with Lisa and Pierre and Evan. And in the way back, I could make out Mr. Allen and Maury Kovalski. They seemed to be spending enough to make up for the broke-ness of the kids. Their whole table was covered with food: those mini-hamburgers called sliders that you can eat if you want to pretend you're a giant, a huge pot of cheese fondue, a platter of nachos the size of my head. It was like they'd ordered everything on the menu.

URP

The show was going to start in a few minutes, so I thought I'd say hello before I went backstage. My stomach was full of butterflies, and I decided chatting was bet-ter than pacing around trying to remember my jokes and imagining what it would feel like to bomb in front of everyone I knew.

"Hi," I said. "Thanks for coming, Mr. Allen. You too, Maury."

Maury shoved calamari into his mouth, wiped away the marinara sauce with the napkin tucked under his chin, and said, "Well, well. Look who it is. The man of the hour. Mr. Big Shot. Fancypants McGillicuddy. Captain Superstar."

High-Falutin' Fondue Forks

Tootle-Toes Twinkle-Top

Biggly-Boss Buffalo-Wings

High-Horse Hankletots

Snooty-Pie Pickle-Puss

Winkie-Waist Waddlewick

Greystoke Poupondrous

Pedicurious Maximus

He scratched his chin with the fork. "What was your name again?"

"Good one," I said.

He picked up a buffalo wing and took a bite. "No, really. I forgot your name."

"Sometimes when I eat my own weight in appetizers, my brain stops working, too," I said.

Maury jerked his thumb at Mr. Allen. "He offered to buy me dinner, so I figured I'd eat for the whole month. Like a camel. I tried to tell ya, kid. Comedy doesn't pay." He picked up a fried pickle and toasted me with it. "Break a leg."

No sooner did he say it than the lights dimmed and the host took the stage. And the next thing I knew, he was saying my name and I was threading my way through the tables and clambering up there myself.

I felt great. Talking to Maury had gotten me loose, taking me out of my own head. It was weird how trading a few wisecracks with that gluttonous old crank made me feel like I was part of something. Like there was some secret brotherhood of comedians, and this was how the guys in it treated each other, and outsiders might find it weird or confusing, but to us it was normal and no big deal.

TRADING WISECRACKS

I took the microphone off the stand and unwrapped the cord, which also made me feel like part of the brotherhood, since it was what every comedian I'd ever seen did. You had to wonder why they wrapped it around the stand to begin with. Maybe it was some kind of union rule or something.

"Hey," I said. "How about a round of applause for the waitresses?" I was kind of surprised to hear myself say it, since my actual opening line was supposed to be about how the baseball season was starting in a few months and I had some ideas about how to make the game more exciting, such as eliminating four players, adding some ten-foot-tall baskets to the field, covering it in parquet, and substituting the hard, small ball for a much larger, bouncier one. But that seemed stale compared to what was actually happening right now, right here, so I went with it. I could always do the baseball joke later.

Everybody applauded—which was amazing in itself, that I could make a whole room of people clap just by asking them to—and when it died down, I gestured at my friends in the front row and said, "That's right, show them some love. It's the least you can do, if you're gonna order one Coke and six straws." That got a laugh. "And no," I continued, "to answer your next question, the salad is not two dollars cheaper if you leave out the avocado, so don't ask."

Since I was talking about food, the next thing to pop into my head was a joke I'd made to Evan a few weeks earlier.

"I'm thinking of opening a restaurant," I said. "Mostly as a way to mess with people. It's going to be a fusion restaurant because those are all the rage now. I'm thinking vegan-pork fusion. Nobody's done that yet. We'd serve dishes like tofu and broccoli stir-fry over brown rice . . . with a pork chop. Or soy-protein nuggets with turnip greens . . . drenched in four gallons of ham gravy. With a side of bacon."

I had to stop and wait until the laughter died down, and when it did I pivoted to a new thing. I was beginning to understand that laughs were more than just the desired result of comedy—just as important was that they broke up your routine, let you move between jokes without awkward transitions.

"The other idea I have for my restaurant is that there'd be two price lists: a regular price list, and a carbon-neutral price list." I waited to let that sink in. "What does it mean? Nobody knows. But who wouldn't pay an extra couple bucks to be carbon neutral?" I paused and pretended to think about it. "Not counting my friends in the front row, who I see just ordered one corn chip and six pairs of tweezers."

"Another thing I'd do at my restaurant? Halfway through your meal, I'd walk up to you and say, 'Hi, I'm the manager. I just wanted to make sure you were enjoying everything.' And when you're like, 'Oh, yeah, this lentil and alfalfa sprout wrap topped with an entire roast pig is delicious,' I'd be like, 'Fantastic, I'm so happy to hear it. And how has the service been?' And when you say, 'Oh, great,' that's when I come a little closer and say, 'Really. You don't think your waitress has been acting a little . . . strange?' And then I come really close, like uncomfortably close,

Price List

	Reg.	C.N.
Wings	12	48-
Egg rolls	8-	72-
Kebab	14	23-
Soup	12	98-
Spam	3-	111-

and I say, 'I think she's stealing from me. I need you to keep an eye out for anything suspicious. And hey, dessert's on me.' And then I walk away. You never see me again. And also, when the check comes, dessert was definitely *not* on me."

The audience roared. I felt so loose and free up there on that stage that I never wanted it to end. Which is probably why I did thirteen minutes instead of the five I was supposed to, as the host informed me when I finally took my bow and floated into the wings on a cloud of applause.

"Sorry," I told him. "I guess I lost track of time."

He slapped me on the back. "Don't worry about it, kid. You killed. You're welcome back anytime."

I felt like a star.

CHAPTER 6

Thursday morning, I leaped out of bed with a pep in my step and a glide in my stride, as my dad likes to say.

He acts like he made that up, but I know he got it from an old funk song, the one about dancing underwater and not getting wet.

I felt like I could do that, too.

I strutted into the kitchen. Lisa was sitting at the table reading the comics. My mom was rushing out the door, her coffee mug in one hand and her briefcase in the other, and my dad was standing at the stove, about to flip a pancake.

I caught it in midair and took a bite. Like some kind of superhero.

"Are you nuts?" my father said. "That pancake is only half-cooked."

Which was true, and now my mouth was full of gloopy batter. The same gloopy batter that was also dripping down my hand and onto my shirt, pants, and shoes.

"Save it for the stage, you bozo," Lisa said without looking up.

"I did that on purpose," I said, trying to save face. "I like them half-cooked." I took another bite to prove it.

They both raised their eyebrows, which is something my father and Lisa do exactly the same way. It was like being silently criticized in surround sound.

"I'm gonna, uh, go change my clothes," I mumbled, and walked out of the room as coolly as I could, considering there was now pancake batter in my shoes.

But even that didn't dampen my mood. I'd still killed last night. People I didn't even know had walked up to me afterward and shaken my hand and said they hadn't laughed so hard all week.

The other comedians talked shop with me in the greenroom while we ate stale M&M's from a chipped dish. Maury Kovalski himself had punched me lightly in the arm and said, "That wasn't half-bad, Jason." Which I figured was high praise, coming from that schlemiel.

And when I walked into home-room, I got a standing ovation. It's true that everyone was standing already because they were gathered around Hotch the snake's cage, watching him gnaw on a leaf of radicchio. But it still counts.

"Our resident comedy genius!" Mr. Allen said. "Jake, how would you like to change the paper in Hotch's cage?"

CHANGING THE paper IN HOTCH's Cage
week 1-Zenobia (Wall St. Journal)
week 2-WHITMAN (New York Times)
week 3-BIN-BIN (Washington Post)
week 4-FORREST (USA Today)
week 5-Jake (National Enquirer)

I guess that was supposed to be an honor or something. Although most honors don't involve the risk of accidentally touching snake poop.

"Okay," I said.

Azure hopped over to me. It took her three hops. "You were so good," she said. "I can't wait till next week."

"Thanks," I said. "Why are you hopping?"

"It's an art project," she said. Which was the

explanation for most weird behavior around here: Azure hopping, Whitman referring to himself in third person, Bin-Bin doing tai chi for an entire day and recording herself with a camera strapped to her wrist. I'd learned to take it in stride.

"Wait a second," I said. "What do you mean, next week? What happens next week?"

She looked puzzled and jumped in place a couple of times. "You. At the Yuk-Yuk. Again."

My mouth fell open but nothing came out. I could feel my ears burning, and the pancake gloop in my stomach suddenly seemed to be expanding at a rapid rate.

"Next week?" I managed at last.

"Yeah, dude. And the week after that, and the week after that." And Azure hopped away, only to turn and hop back a second later. "You're still coming to my dance recital this afternoon, right?"

"Uh-huh," I muttered. But I was busy realizing the problem with being a star.

Because what do stars do? They fall.

OTHER THINGS THAT FALL

ROME

HUMPTY DUMPTY

Leaves in October

Staying up there in the sky requires a ton of energy. And this particular star had burned through ninety percent of his material last night.

I couldn't get up there next week and tell the same jokes.

And I couldn't *not* get up there next week. I had fans now.

This was probably why comedians went on tour. Switching audiences is easier than switching jokes.

Which, in turn, was probably why so few comedians were in middle school.

"Hey," said Forrest, breaking me out of my panic attack. "You were funny last night. For a human being, anyway."

The panic was still racing around inside me, like some kind of deranged ferret. I couldn't let the ferret get the best of me, so I turned to Forrest and said, "Of course I was. I'm Jake Liston, man. The funniest dude alive."

I felt more like *Jake Liston, totally incapable of ever*

being funny again, but when I said it, the ferret stopped clawing at my small intestine for a moment.

You know what they say: *Fake it till you make it.* Maybe if I acted like the world's greatest and most successful comic, the jokes would come and the panic ferret would go to sleep. It was worth a try.

I cleared my throat and cupped my hands around my mouth like a bullhorn.

"People!" I shouted. "Could I have your attention, please?" They all turned away from their instruments and books and whatever else they were fiddling with. Even Mr. Allen put down his didgeridoo and cocked his head at me.

"I'd just like to thank you all for coming out to support me last night," I said, and everybody started to smile. "I couldn't do it without the fans. The little people. I'll never forget you, no matter how rich and famous I become."

There was a moment of silence. Then Klaus started applauding madly. Everybody looked at him. He didn't notice, or maybe he didn't care. He kept on clapping for a full minute, even after everybody else had gone back to what they were doing.

"Uh, thanks," I said when he finally stopped. Nobody responded. I sensed a chill in the room. Which was unusual, since the room was a tropical rain forest.

Maybe it was *Fake it till you break it.*

"Time for English," Mr. Allen announced, interrupting my thoughts. "Get out your notebooks or write on your arms. Today we're looking at the epic poem in world literature."

Before the development of writing, epic poems were **memorized** & played an important part in maintaining a record of the great deeds & history of a culture!!

Great deeds? Kinda like my epic set last night!!

Lucky for me, that was so boring that the ferret stayed asleep the whole rest of the morning.

• • •

Lunch that day was chanterelle mushroom fettuccine and spinach-walnut-gorgonzola salad. But when I got my tray and went to sit down, Zenobia and Bin-Bin scooted into the empty space at the table.

"Sorry, Jake," Zenobia said. "This table is just for the *little people*."

"We wouldn't want to disturb your genius comedy brain," Bin-Bin added. "Not when you have jokes to think up."

"Plus," added Whitman, "it can be such a burden to always have to deal with fans."

"Okaaaay," I said slowly. "I guess I'll just . . . sit over here, then." I walked over to an empty table.

I was pretty sure they were being sarcastic, but the truth was, some alone time sounded good. I did have to think of some jokes. Especially since a good portion of my week was now going to be spent writing the epic rhyming poem Mr. Allen had just assigned us.

I sat there all period, racking my brain and shoveling food into my face. Soon my stomach was full, but my notebook was still empty. And the ferret of panic had woken up from his nap and was drinking a triple espresso and kicking me behind the eyeballs with his spiky little clawed feet. He was a real jerk.

That night, I locked myself in my room to work on my routine. It went something like this:

1. Stare at blank page. (5 minutes)

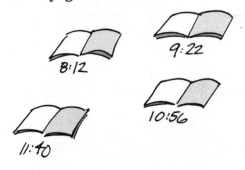

2. Have thought: "Bears are funny." (3 seconds)
3. Try to think of joke about bears. (3 minutes)

4. Type "bears funny" into YouTube. (4 seconds)

5. Watch YouTube videos of bears paddling around in aboveground swimming pools, eating barbecue, destroying campgrounds, wearing sombreros, and being chased by cats. (47 minutes)

6. Wonder why Winnie-the-Pooh, and for that matter so many other cartoon characters, always wears a shirt but no pants. Why is this acceptable fashion? (1 minute)

7. Write joke about Winnie-the-Pooh and Donald Duck going pants shopping and thinking all the pants make them look fat and not buying anything. (3 minutes)

8. Triumphant cookie break (11 minutes)

9. Try and fail to write any other bear jokes. Consider placing plate of cookies outside so bears will come eat cookies and maybe do something funny I can write joke about. (1 minute)

10. Remember I live in non-bear-infested area. (30 seconds)

11. Decide bears are maybe not that funny after all. (10 seconds)

ITEMS LESS FUNNY THAN BEARS

DRYER LINT

A COPY OF "RETURN TO OZ" ON LASERDISC (ask your mom)

A quarter PINT of local Bodega Potato salad

A used Q-Tip

12. Decide only things less funny than bears are
    a) death by piranha and b) Jake Liston.
    (15 seconds)
13. Decide weasels are funny. (1 minute)
14. Write joke about weasels secretly controlling
    U.S. government. (4 minutes)
15. Erase stupid U.S. government weasel joke.
    (4 seconds)
16. Sad cookie break #2 (9 minutes)

17. Call Evan to ask if weasels are funny. Find out
    from Evan's older brother that Evan is at the
    championship game of his indoor soccer league.

Remember that I promised to attend.
(2 minutes)

18. Remember that I also promised to go to Azure's dance performance, which is also right now. (1 minute)
19. Self-hating lasagna break (12 minutes)
20. Depressed cookie break #3 (6 minutes)
21. Feel sick. (21 minutes)
22. Bathroom break (7 minutes)
23. Jot down single decent joke that came to me in bathroom, about how every time I enter a public restroom I am in deadly fear that there is already someone in there who has neglected to lock the door, even though this has never actually happened. (2 minutes)
24. Pass out fully clothed. (8 hours)

It was not exactly a productive evening. But it wasn't until the next morning that I realized just how badly I had used my time.

CHAPTER 7

I was having a dream about super-intelligent bear-riding weasels stealing all the toilet paper in the world and handing it over to their ferret overlords, when the phone rang.

I ignored it, since I never get calls early in the morning, but the next thing I heard was Mom yelling, "Jake! Phone!" I wish people in my family took the time to actually walk into the same room as the people they want to talk to, but that almost never happens. We'll have family conversations from four different rooms sometimes, and I'm just as bad about it as anybody.

I picked up the phone and said, "Jake Liston is asleep. Please leave a message."

"Where were you yesterday?" Evan asked. His voice sounded tight, like a coiled-up snake.

"Sorry, dude," I said, rubbing the sleep out of my eyes. "I got caught up trying to write some new jokes. I'm really stressed out about performing next week, and I—"

"I came to see you do your thing," Evan interrupted. "And you were supposed to come see me do mine."

He was right, and I knew I probably should have been apologizing, but something about the way he sounded rubbed me wrong. Like I was supposed to drop everything just to watch him kick a ball around. Didn't he understand how seriously I was trying to take this comedy thing?

STUFF I MISSED DURING EVAN'S SOCCER MATCH

BOOT

EVAN BEING SHOWN A YELLOW CARD BEFORE THE MATCH EVEN STARTS!!

EVAN "MISTAKENLY" KICKING REF INSTEAD OF BALL!!

EVAN TAUNTING OPPOSING PLAYERS WHILST BEING REMOVED FROM PITCH!!

EVAN BEING SHOWN A RED CARD BEFORE HALFTIME!!

"I said I was sorry," I answered, knowing my voice was as tight as his now, and that I sounded extremely not sorry. "But I had urgent stuff to do. I need to have all-new material by next Thursday."

All I heard over the line was quiet. But it was a very loud, angry kind of quiet, if you know what I mean.

"Hello?" I said after a while. I knew he was there, but I was sick of waiting.

"You think you're hot stuff now, huh, Jake?" Evan said. "A few weeks ago, you were afraid of getting discovered as a fake and kicked out of school, and now you're too important to come to my game."

I could feel the heat coming off my body, the tightness spreading from my voice down into my chest.

"I don't think I'm hot stuff," I said. "I *know* I'm hot stuff."

And I hung up.

It wasn't true at all. I was cold stuff. Lukewarm stuff at best.

If I'd really felt like hot stuff, I wouldn't have been acting so high and mighty. There are a lot of ways to be a fake, I guess. When I got into Music and Art Academy, I'd been faking that I deserved to be there, pretending I had talent.

Now I'd found something I was actually good at, something that was true to who I really was, and here I was faking being a stuck-up jerk. It was like I was watching myself act like a total punk, but I was powerless to stop it. As if aliens from outer space had taken over my body and were controlling it with some kind of video game joystick.

Alien #1: Hey, now that we have taken total control of this sixth-grade loser, how about we ruin his life for no reason whatsoever?

Alien #2: Ha ha! Yeah! Let's do it! How?

Alien #1: What if we make him kick his teacher in a very sensitive region of his body? Or force him to eat an entire giganto bag of Tootsie Rolls until he starts puking up sticky dark brown puke?

Alien #2: Too obvious. I have a better idea. Let's make him say a bunch of arrogant, jerky stuff he doesn't mean and tick off all his friends.

Alien #1: I like it! But can we also have him write a bunch of stupid jokes about pantsless cartoon characters and public restrooms that no one will find the least bit funny?

Alien #2: I don't see why not. Ha ha ha!

By the time I got to school, the aliens had perfected their technique. As soon as I walked into the homeroom rain forest, Azure hopped up to me with a sad look on her face and said, "Where were you? I looked all over."

Normally, knowing I had let her down would have felt like getting stabbed right in the gut. But not today, because the aliens had placed a reinforced steel plate in my gut so I wouldn't feel a thing.

"I got busy," I said. "I had to write my set."

Her face fell. "But it was my big recital," she said, and her lower lip quivered like she was going to cry.

Alien #1: Yes! Here come the tears! He's being such a tool! High five!

Alien #2: Now let's make him rip a humongous fart.

Alien #1: What a fantastic idea.

But the aliens were wrong. Azure's lip stopped quivering, and suddenly her face looked like it was made of granite.

"Friendship is a two-way street, Jake," she said. And before I could say anything back, she turned on her heel and hopped away. She didn't speak to me for the rest of the day.

Neither, come to think of it, did anybody else.

On Monday, it was the same thing. Except more so. Like, if their not talking to me had been a lasagna, on day one the layer of cheese on top would have been soft and melty. By Tuesday, the cheese was all hard and crusty, and you couldn't cut through it without a knife.

By Wednesday, you would have needed a chainsaw, and I walked around all day feeling like I might burst into tears at any moment.

I couldn't take much more of this. I needed help to climb my way out of the hole I'd dug, and I could think of only one person who might understand what I was going through.

So after school I rode my bike straight to Willow Greens Retirement Home and banged on Maury Kovalski's door.

"Whaddaya want?" I heard a muffled voice shout.

"Advice!" I shouted back.

"Here's some advice!" he shouted. "If you have a bad taste in your mouth, eat some orange peel. Also, never buy gemstones online! And don't play cards with anybody named after a city—or worse, a state!"

Morrisville Midge

Flea Hill Finnegan

Handsome Eddy Edward

He paused for a moment, then said, "Who is this, anyway?"

"Jake Liston!" I shouted back.

"Oh. Hey, kiddo. I was thinking about you earlier. I was watching a TV program about coal miners in the Appalachians in the 1920s."

"Why did that make you think about me?" I shouted.

"Because it was boring!" he shouted. "Kind of like you."

"Real nice talk!" I shouted. "Hey, here's a crazy idea. How about we keep talking, only not on opposite sides of this door? It might be easier on our vocal cords."

The door opened, and Maury peered down at me. He was wearing the same bathrobe as before, and holding a jar with a fork sticking out of it.

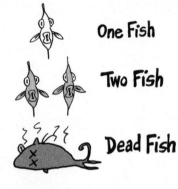

One Fish

Two Fish

Dead Fish

"Come on in, buddy boy," he said. "I was just eating some gefilte fish.

Gefilte Fish

The absolute worst food on earth. You gotta drown it in horseradish, or you'll choke on the miserable stuff."

He waved the jar at me, and I peered inside and saw these beige chunks suspended in what looked like translucent slime. I squinted at the list of ingredients. Apparently gefilte fish wasn't a fish, but a kind of fish log made of carp, pike, and a bunch of other ingredients.

"So why do you eat it?" I asked.

Maury shook his head in exasperation. "Why do I eat it, he asks. Boy, you really are a schlemiel. I eat it because my father ate it, and his father before him, all the way back to the beginning of time. Tradition, boy-o. Tradition." He set the jar down. "So. What kind of advice are you looking for, or did I pretty much cover it already?"

I cleared some space on Maury's couch by pushing aside a stack of record albums, books, and magazines, and sat down.

"Ever since my gig . . . ," I started, and then sighed. "I don't know, Maury. I haven't been myself."

"Let me guess," he said, stabbing a piece of gefilte fish with the fork. With his other hand, he reached into his bathrobe pocket, where he had a jar of horseradish, and smeared some on the gefilte fish with a spoon. Then he shoveled the whole thing in his mouth, and winced. "Wow, that's bad. I'm glad I only do this once a year."

I waited while he chewed and swallowed.

Jake's usual self

Who Jake's been lately

"Let me guess," he said again.

"Who's stopping you?"

He wagged a finger at me. "You let it go to your head and started acting like some kinda big shot, didn't you?"

"How'd you know?" I asked, genuinely surprised.

"Because, kid. It happens to the best of us. Well, maybe not the best. But it happened to me. Have a seat, and I'll tell you a story."

"I am sitting," I pointed out.

"Then stand," he said. I ignored that.

"Picture it," Maury Kovalski went on. "I'm a promising young comedian. Mainly, I'm promising to pay my rent. And my comedy partner and best friend is a guy by the name of Little Abie Mendelson. You know why they called him that?"

"Because his name was Abie Mendelson and he was little?"

"You catch on fast. So anyway, me and Little Abie, we had this whole routine. It was called the Spaceman and the Martian. Abie played the spaceman, and the concept was that he discovers me, the Martian, living in a cave on Mars, and interviews me about my life. Mostly, it was improvised. But we had the magic. He knew what I was gonna say before I did, so he knew how to set me up. And I knew how to drop hints, so he'd ask me the right questions. We were like Kevin Durant and Russell Westbrook, sonny boy."

The breakup has been devastating!! Durant & Westbrook were known as the "Maury Kovalski & Abie Mendelson of basketball"!!

CHANNEL 11 SPORTS
OKLAHOMIE's #1 SNOOZECAST!!

"Sounds like you got to be a lot funnier than he did," I said, after getting over my surprise that Maury Kovalski followed basketball.

He snapped his fingers around the fork. This caused a bunch of juice to shoot out of the piece of gefilte fish on the fork and splatter against the floor.

"Exactly," Maury said. "He was the straight man, to use a comedy term. Just as important a part of the routine, but a lot less glamorous. And so naturally, people focused on me, because I was the one getting laughs. Pretty soon, people wanted to book the Martian on TV shows, where there was no room for the Spaceman because the host wanted to do the interview himself. And what did I do?"

Maury sighed, and all of a sudden he looked much older and sadder.

"What?" I asked.

"I said yes. I let the attention go to my head, and I left Little Abie Mendelson in the lurch. I forgot about the most important thing in life—friendship."

"So what happened to Abie?"

"We haven't spoken in almost fifty years."

"And the Martian?"

Maury shrugged. "I had a good little run. But it wasn't as funny without Abie. And it wasn't as fun. So I retired the character. And here I am."

Maury pointed his fork at me. "Don't make the same mistake I did, kiddo. Fix things with your friends."

I knew he was right.

"How?" I asked.

"I gotta do everything around here? Figure it out yourself."

"I'll get right to work on it," I said, forgetting entirely that before I could, I had to write an epic rhyming poem that was due tomorrow.

HOW TO FIX THINGS WITH YOUR FRIENDS*

(IN 3 easy steps!!)
WHaT YOU'LL NEED:

A HaMMeR

ONe boTTLe of NONTOXiC gLue

2 OUNCeS of APPLe CIDeR ViNeGaR

ONe BaNaNa

(* If ONLY iT weRe THiS easy!!)

CHAPTER 8

The Land of Splattamere

AN EPIC POEM BY GEFILTE JAKE LISTON

In a faraway land that was called Splattamere
Things were quite different from how they are here.

In everyday life, things were always absurd.

Goofballs were everywhere. Popular words
In Splattamere included booger *and* poophead.

SPLATTAMERE'S TOP-TEN WORDS

1. KRINKLEBUNZ
2. DINGBAT
3. BOOGER
4. HAMMY HAMTOES
5. DIZZY GILLESPIE
6. POOPHEAD
7. GOOBANZO BEAN
8. FINKLEPUSS
9. NUMBSKULL
10. KRICFALUSI

The most common disease was to laugh yourself dead.
Nobody walked down the street without tripping
And landing headfirst in a coop full of chickens.
No one had names like Sam Jones or Ray Smith.

Instead, they had names like Amanda Huggenkiss.
In school, every five seconds somebody farted
So nobody got any lessons imparted.
The situation sounds cool but it was unbearable.
Yogurt and soup always ended up wearable.
And every time somebody tried to be serious
Some kind of shenanigans made him delirious.
The people were laughed out, exhausted and tired.
And then one fine day, a kid got inspired.
He had an idea that changed things forever.
His name was Gefilte, and he was quite clever.
He said to himself, Everything is so funny.
If someone was serious, people'd pay money
To sit and not laugh, just to have an escape
From the constant hilarity we always face.

READING MATERIAL FOR
THE SERIOUS ROUTINE

INGREDIENT LIST
ON A GIRL SCOUT
COOKIE BOX

OXFORD
DICTIONARY

APPLIANCE
MANUAL

So Gefilte sat down and he wrote some material
About weather and paperwork, Scotch tape and cereal.

He made it all boring and simple and plain.
And when it was all just insanely mundane
He got a microphone, then built a stage
And memorized everything on every page.
And then he put signs up all over the town
That said "On Thursday night, kindly come down
To Gefilte's house—prepare to be bored to death
By an evening of guaranteed seriousness."
He wondered all week if the townsfolk would come.
But on Thursday night, it turned out that everyone
In Splattamere had packed themselves into his basement.
He looked down and wondered where all of the space went.
And they looked back up at him desperate to hear
Something unfunny, and soon a big cheer
Erupted, for the first un-joke Gefilte delivered
Was so lame that the crowd gasped, and then they shivered.
Not one single giggle escaped from their throats
As Gefilte rambled pointlessly on about oats.

ZZZZ

ZZZ

=snore=

96% ON
BORINGTOMATOES.COM!

"SO BORING, HE PUT A WHOLE
HERD OF RED BULLS TO SLEEP!!"

Then he switched subjects and told them a story
About ballpoint pens that made everyone snorey.
The crowd ate it up. They loved every minute.
They hung on each word—they were totally in it.

Gefilte could feel the room's boredom increasing.
The pressure of their lives was slowly releasing.
And by the time he stepped down off of the stage
Gefilte's new stand-up act was all the rage.
The people of Splattamere, with all their might
Begged him to perform again the next night

And the next and the next, and the next and the next
To counter the laughter that had them so vexed.
And from that day on, Gefilte was known
As the pride of the town, for inventing his own
Way of providing the lameness they craved
The only thing that kept the people behaved.
"Hurray for Gefilte," the townsfolk all cried.
"Hurray for the night that the laughter died."
And that, my fine friends, is the end of the story.
I hope you all found it unbearably borey.

CHAPTER 9

Writing my epic poem pretty much wiped me out, and I sleepwalked through the next day of school.

But it was more of the same. Azure hopped right by me without stopping, like some kind of snooty kangaroo. In gym class, I booted a grand slam in kickball, and nobody said a word or high-fived me or anything.

At lunch, I didn't even try to sit with my friends, because I was pretty sure they'd give me the cold shoulder.

Instead, I took my tray back to the rain forest and ate with Hotch, the snake. Even she seemed to be acting kind of weird toward me.

I knew I had to make it right, like Maury Kovalski said. A regular apology didn't feel like enough. I wanted to do something big, something spectacular. Something that would show everybody that I understood taking comedy seriously didn't mean I was allowed to be a huge jerk-face.

The only problem was, I had no idea what that something was.

I got off the school bus and walked home slowly, mulling it over. But when I turned onto my block, I noticed that something a little strange was going on.

More specifically, I noticed that there were approximately seven hundred thousand million people standing on the street and the sidewalk and my front lawn. Half of them were holding microphones, and the other half were pointing cameras at the ones holding microphones. Trucks were parked everywhere, with things like "KPDC NEWS" and "GOOD MORNING AMERICA" and "TOKYO EXPRESS" and "HELLO NEW ZEALAND" printed on the sides, and satellite dishes attached to the tops.

Before I could ask what was going on, the reporter closest to me, a woman wearing a red blazer and a ton of makeup, said, "Okay, Charlie—action!" and started talking in a loud, perky, morning-show-type voice.

Reporter: We're here outside the home of Lisa Liston, one-half of the scorching-hot new group Conceptual Art Band, whose song "The Ballad of the Duck-Billed Platypus" has come out of nowhere to take the Internet by storm.

Me: (*Gasps, swallows the wrong way, proceeds to cough and choke uncontrollably for twenty seconds. Recovers. Screams.*) WHAT?

Reporter: Cut! Charlie, this kid coughed all over my intro. Let's try it again. (*to me*) Beat it, huh, kid? She's not signing any autographs today.

Me: WHAT IS HAPPENING RIGHT NOW?

Reporter: What's happening is, I'm trying to tape a piece about the hottest band in the world, and you're standing next to me barfing up a lung. Now, please, can I do my job? (*Hip-checks me out of the way* *and turns back to the camera.)* Very little is known about Conceptual Art Band. The members, Lisa Liston and Pierre Le Crucet, have not given any interviews since their video debuted earlier today, racking up twenty-five million YouTube views in less than three hours. In fact, it's possible that they don't even know how famous they are. . . .

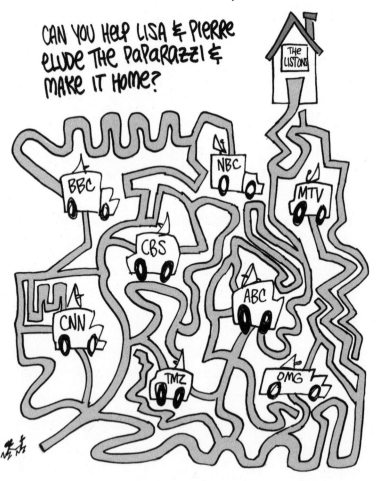

It was too much. I staggered up the front walk and slipped into the house. The reporters didn't seem to notice that I actually lived there. They were too busy foaming at the mouth.

"Hi," I called out, nice and casual, from the front hall. "I'm home! Mr. Allen really liked my epic poem. I kicked a grand slam in kickball today. And oh, by the way, the entire news media of the entire world is camped out on our front lawn. Do we have any cookies?"

Lisa rushed up to me, her face flushed all red like she'd been leaning over a campfire.

"I know!" she said. "It's pretty gnarly, right?"

Pierre sauntered in behind her, slurping on a Popsicle. "Pretty weird, right, C3P-Bro? We've been trying to figure out how it happened." He took his phone out of his pocket and frowned at it. "I mean, sure, Taylor Swift and Prince Charles both tweeted about it, but that was, like, *after* it blew up, so . . ." He shrugged and took another slurp. "Who knows. Cool beans, though. Whatever."

I looked at them both. "How are you guys so calm? There are a million reporters out there. Are you gonna talk to them?"

Lisa shrugged. "Maybe tomorrow. I kinda just feel like chilling right now."

"It's cooler if we wait," Pierre agreed. "Plus, we should probably write another song."

"Conceptual Art Band doesn't have any other songs?"

"Not any good ones," Lisa said. "We've only had this band for like three weeks, Bro-am Chomsky."

"Do Mom and Dad know?" I asked.

PIERRE'S 4 TYPES OF MOODS

CHILL

DOWN-TEMPO

UNFAZED

MELANCHOLIC

"What, that we have no other good songs?"

"No, that 'The Ballad of the Duck-Billed Platypus' has twenty-five million views on YouTube in the last three hours!"

Pierre checked his phone. "Twenty-eight million," he updated me.

"I called Mom at work," Lisa replied. "She was psyched. But it didn't mean that much to her. She and Dad don't understand YouTube. Not that I do, either, really . . ." She reached into the fridge, pulled out a slice of leftover pizza, and took a giant bite. "We did get a cool email from the Society for the Appreciation of the Duck-Billed Platypus, though. That was rad."

"And we're making a nice chunk of change," Pierre added. "From YouTube ads or whatever. Also, two movies and a TV show want to use the song."

WHAT MAKES $$$$ ON YOUTUBE

KITTY VIDEOS

KITTY WITH CUCUMBER VIDEO

POST MORE KITTY VIDS!!

THE FAT CAT THAT OWNS YOUTUBE

Lisa shoved her hand in her pocket and pulled out a roll of money. "Here," she said, peeling off some crisp bills and shoving them at me. "That's for you. For being in the video."

I counted the wad. "This is eight hundred dollars, guys."

"Yup," said Pierre. "The movie people literally delivered us a briefcase full of cash. Enjoy it, dude." He grinned. "I bought myself a Porsche."

"A Porsche! How did you buy a Porsche? *When* did you buy a Porsche? Your song only blew up three hours ago!"

"I bought it online, Martin Van Bro-ren. They're gonna deliver it tomorrow. No muss, no fuss." He made a hand-wiping motion and grinned a big idiotic grin at me.

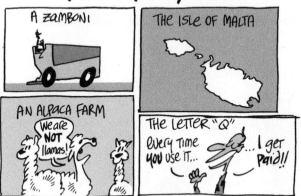

I stared uncomprehendingly at both of them, the way a manatee might stare at the Theory of Relativity. "This is a lot to process," I said.

"Totally," Lisa agreed. "Take your time. I'm going to make some popcorn and watch the reporters from the upstairs window."

"Oh, man!" said Pierre. "Popcorn! That's a great idea." He checked his phone again. "Twenty-nine million," he said. "Can we put Caesar salad dressing on the popcorn?"

"Absolutely," said Lisa.

She made the popcorn, which was weirdly delicious with Caesar dressing, and I went upstairs with them.

For the next couple of hours we just sat there, watching the reporters mill around and talk into the cameras.

"I wonder how long they'll stay," I whispered.

"Until we talk to them," Pierre said.

"Watch this," said Lisa. She opened the window, leaned outside, and waved.

"Hi!" she yelled. All the camera dudes scrambled to catch it, and all the reporters lifted their microphones and started screaming questions.

Lisa closed the window and giggled.

Eventually, my mom and dad came home with Chinese food. They snuck in the back door to avoid the media, and the five of us ate in front of the upstairs window, shoveling the food straight from the cartons into our faces, which normally my parents would have disapproved of. But we were all too mesmerized by the hullabaloo to bother with manners.

"They're not going to sleep here, are they?" my mother asked. "Maybe I should bring them some blankets."

"You two need to talk to a professional," my father declared, pointing his chopsticks at Lisa and Pierre.

"You mean like a shrink?" I said.

"A manager," he said. "An entertainment attorney. Maybe a financial planner. You've got to maximize this opportunity while you can. I'll ask Uncle Rory."

Lisa rolled her eyes. "Uncle Rory is a mailman, Dad."

"In Beverly Hills! He knows all kinds of big stars."

"Whatever, Dad. Does this mean you guys are on board with me taking a year off before college?"

My parents exchanged a glance, and then my mom said, "We'll discuss it."

Which is their way of saying yes without saying it. Lisa grinned and offered me a high five. I slapped her palm, which was a little greasy from duck sauce.

3 THINGS YOU WON'T FIND IN DUCK SAUCE
1. Vitamins
2. Minerals
3. Duck

The excitement took its toll on us, and by nine-thirty we were all ready for bed. Pierre slept on the couch in the basement rather than risk going outside.

But when I lay down, all the craziness over Conceptual Art Band drifted out of my mind, like clouds when the wind picks up, and I remembered that I had a problem to solve. I had to make things right with my friends.

I still wasn't sure how to do it, but now I had something I hadn't had before: eight hundred bucks. And just like that, an idea hit me. What if I rented out the Yuk-Yuk, invited everybody who was mad at me, and threw a Friend Appreciation Night? I could pull out all the stops to show them how sorry I was and how much they meant to me.

If I could convince them to come, anyway.

CHAPTER 10

On Friday, we all had to sneak out the back door to get to school and work without getting pounced on by the media—which had not stayed overnight but was back bright and early, clogging up our whole block. The neighbors had started to call and complain, and my dad spent half the morning apologizing for all the noise and traffic, and promising that we'd do our best to get rid of them as soon as possible, and offering everybody free tickets to see Conceptual Art Band whenever they actually got it together to play a show.

MATCH THE "SORRY" TO THE LANGUAGE IT'S FROM!!

"VABANDUST"
"ENTSCHULDIGUNG"
"SORRY"
"JAMMER"
"FAKAMOLEMOLE"
"UNDSKYLD"
"NGIYAXOLISA"
"SAMAHANI"
"ANTEEKSI"
"PATAWAD"

DANISH
ESTONIA
SWAHILI
TAGALOG
FINNISH
ZULU
ENGLISH
TONGAN
AFRIKAAN
GERMAN

Lisa and Pierre wore disguises for added protection, even though the reporters didn't actually know what they looked like, except for Lisa's arm. The only disguises on hand were a bunch of old Halloween costumes, so Lisa went to school dressed as a Cruella De Vil from *101 Dalmatians*, and Pierre went as Colonel Sanders. He kept making jokes in a bad Southern accent about drinking gravy, like "Ah onleh care about two thangs: wearin' bolo ties an' drinkin' giant amounts ah graaaveh!" which Lisa thought were hilarious and I got sick of after a few minutes.

I still couldn't believe how relaxed they both seemed, as if getting 43 million YouTube views and suddenly being famous was no big deal at all. It also made me realize even more what a toolbox I had been to think my little stand-up set at the Yuk-Yuk made me some kind of big shot who could afford to act all snooty. I mean, if worldwide fame wasn't going to their heads, why should a few laughs go to mine?

I called the manager of the Yuk-Yuk before school and arranged to rent it out on Friday night. So by the time we got to M&AA, I had a stack of invitations to hand out to everybody. Starting with Azure.

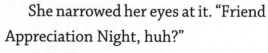

Stack o' invites

I walked up and handed her one.

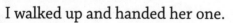

She narrowed her eyes at it. "Friend Appreciation Night, huh?"

"Yeah," I said.

"Uh-huh," she said, turning her narrowed eyes at me.

"It's my way of apologizing," I explained.

"So . . . to prove that you're sorry for turning into a jerk the last time we came and laughed at your jokes, you're asking us to come and laugh at your jokes again?"

I hadn't quite thought of it like that, and so on the spot I made a decision. "I'm not going to tell any jokes," I said. "I just want to show my friends how important they are."

Azure handed me back the invitation. "You don't have to do all this, Jake. An apology is good enough."

"Conceptual Art Band is going to play," I told her.

Azure screamed at the top of her lungs for about twenty-five seconds.

* Not responsible for glassware that may have broken from this scream

Twenty-five seconds is not a long time usually. But when someone is screaming at the top of her lungs, it feels like an eternity.

"They're my favorite band in the world!" she told me, panting, when she stopped. "I watched their video like fifty times last night! How in the world did you get them?"

"Uh . . . you know Conceptual Art Band is just my sister and Pierre, right? And that's me and Evan in the video, dressed like eggs."

Azure screwed up her face. "Really?"

"Yeah, dude. You watched the video fifty times and you didn't recognize any of us?"

Azure looked puzzled. "Were you wearing makeup or something?"

"Well, Lisa and Pierre have wigs on. And you can't see much more than Evan's and my legs. But it's us."

"Holy cow. Your sister's famous, man."

"I know. So you'll come?"

"I'll come. But not because of Conceptual Art Band."

"That's—" I started to say, but Azure hugged me so hard I couldn't breathe.

"You're a good egg, Jake," she said when she let go. "And I don't just mean in the video." Then she walked away.

HOW DO YOU LIKE YOUR EGGS?

RUNNY?

AUGH!!

CRACKED?

=HIC=

PICKLED?

POACHED?

They only wanted us for our shells!!

By lunch (goat cheese and roasted bell pepper frittata, sunchoke soup), I had handed out the invitations, and the room had definitely thawed, in terms of how my friends were treating me. I was still sensing a hint of skepticism from Bin-Bin and Zenobia and a few others, probably because, like Azure said, it was a little weird to apologize for being full of myself by inviting everybody back to the place where I'd gotten that way. But maybe there was also something appropriate about it.

There were two things I still had to do. One was plan the entertainment for the evening, besides asking Conceptual Art Band to perform. I had some ideas about that. It wasn't going to be easy, and it would probably take all the money I had left after renting the Yuk-Yuk, but I thought I could pull it off.

The second and more difficult thing was apologizing to Evan and making sure he came. I'd been the jerkiest to him by far, and Evan was kind of a stubborn guy.

JeRK
CHicKeN

JeRK
SHrimp

PLain
jerk

For example, when we were in second grade, we'd had a contest to see who could wear the same shirt longer. I think we bet, like, fifty cents or something, which was a lot of money back then. Not only did Evan win, but just to prove a point he wore the shirt for an additional two weeks after the contest was over. He kept it hidden under a can of motor oil in his garage, and after he left the house for school every morning, he'd sneak in there and put it on. By the end, it was covered in so many food stains that he probably could have survived a week in the wilderness just by sucking on it. The point being, once Evan sets his mind on something, changing it is not the easiest thing. But he was my oldest friend and I had to try, so I went straight to his house after school and rang the bell.

His mom answered. Her name is Celia. She's almost like my second mom, I've spent so much time at Evan's house.

"Jake. Hi." She looked surprised to see me, which probably meant that Evan had told her about our fight.

"Hi," I said. "Is Evan home?"

She opened her mouth, then closed it again, then opened it. "He is." Long pause. "I'm sorry, Jake. He saw you coming up the walk, and he told me

137

to tell you he doesn't want to see you." It looked like it was breaking her heart to say it.

"Oh," I said, feeling my own heart crack open a little.

"I'm sorry, sweetie. You know how he can be. But I'm sure he'll come around. Is there anything you want me to tell him?"

VooDoo DoLL evan made!!

"Tell him I'm sorry for missing his game," I said. "And that I know friendship is a two-way street, and I won't forget it again. And tell him he should come to this." I handed her the last invitation to Friend Appreciation Night.

"I will," she said.

"Thanks. Oh, and tell him that my sister has a

bunch of money for him, from the video. I don't know if you heard, but the song kind of blew up."

"I sure did!" Evan's mom said. She looked at the invitation. "I'll give this to him right now, Jake."

She waved goodbye and shut the door. I stood there for a few seconds, staring at the closed door. Then I looked up at Evan's bedroom window and waved, just in case he was watching.

CHAPTER 11

Nobody except the invited guests was supposed to know that Conceptual Art Band was playing at the Yuk-Yuk, but somehow word got out. When we arrived to load in all their equipment, there were about four dozen reporters waiting, and this time there was no avoiding them.

WHERE ARE THEY NOW?

THOSE EGGS FROM THAT C.A.B. VIDEO:

I USED TQ be somebody!!

FIFI'S FIFTIES DINER

"I guess it's time to talk," Lisa said to Pierre.

"Uh-huh," he agreed. "Let's do it." They high-fived and turned to face the throng.

"Howdy," Lisa said. "So, uh, we're Conceptual Art Band. I'm Lisa, and this is my boyfriend, Pierre."

"Hi," said Pierre. "I'm Pierre, and this is my girl-friend, Lisa. We're Conceptual Art Band."

The reporters all started screaming questions at once: How does it feel to have a hit? Why the duck-billed platypus? What's next for the band? Blah blah blah. Considering how long Lisa and Pierre had made them wait, I thought they'd come up with more inter-esting questions.

Apparently, Lisa agreed. "No offense," she said, "but those are all pretty boring questions. Can't we talk about something else?"

"Yeah," said Pierre. "I mean, we don't really know what's next. But you know what's fascinating? Mushrooms. Did you know that there are mushrooms underground that are miles long? They're the big-gest life-forms on the planet. Isn't that cool?"

FUN FACT: MARS IS CALLED THE RED PLANET BECAUSE ITS SURFACE IS COVERED IN A MILD MARINARA SAUCE.

The reporters didn't really know what to make of that. I guess they were used to bands wanting to talk about themselves.

"Super cool," said Lisa. "Hey, you know what that reminds me of? The weight of all the ants in the world is equal to the weight of all the humans. Crazy, right?"

"No way," said Pierre.

"Yes way," said Lisa.

"Far out," said Pierre.

"Without a doubt, Cub Scout," said Lisa.

"Shout, don't pout," said Pierre.

"About grout, you lout," said Lisa.

The reporters were quiet. I think they weren't really sure what was going on. Maybe they suspected that they were watching some sort of conceptual art piece right now. But I knew that was just how Pierre and Lisa talked.

Finally, we all managed to get inside. There were a lot of Conceptual Art Band fans lined up outside, too, but when the club manager told them this was a private show, they started to drift away.

Pretty soon after that, my friends started to arrive. They took their seats, and I went around greeting everyone. All the food was on the house, and the waitresses brought out a ton of appetizers for everybody, until all the tables looked like Maury's and Mr. Allen's had last week. Speaking of Mr. Allen, he showed up, too, along with my whole class, my parents, and a bunch of Lisa's and Pierre's buddies. It turned out that after a few crazy days of fame, they felt like they needed to show some appreciation for their friends, too, for keeping them sane in the middle of all the madness. Which was fine by me. The crowd was rounded out by some of the disgruntled neighbors my dad had promised tickets to. They weren't disgruntled anymore. In fact, they were totally gruntled.

When everybody was stuffed full of delicious,

unhealthy comedy club food, I jumped onstage and grabbed the mic.

"Welcome to Friend Appreciation Night!" I howled. "I'm your host, Jake Liston, and tonight I will not be performing. I'm only up here for one reason: to tell you guys that from now on, I'm gonna be the best friend I can to each and every one of you. Last week you all came out to support me, and what did I do? I took it for granted. I didn't pay it back. I—"

"Enough already!" shouted Azure. "We forgive you, dude. Now stop being boring, and tell some jokes or something."

Everybody whooped and hollered, and I figured the point had been made. And that maybe going on and on about it was actually just as egotistical as anything I'd done all week.

"I have something better than jokes," I said.

"There's nothing better than jokes," somebody called back. I wasn't sure who, and the stage lights made it hard to see. Maybe Forrest, although it was hard to imagine him shouting like that.

In any case, I reckoned I'd better tell a couple, at least. "Okay," I said, "I was just going to introduce my sister and her boyfriend, otherwise known as Conceptual Art Band"—the crowd exploded into cheers, and I had to wait it out—"but I guess I can tell you a little about what it's like when somebody you live with suddenly becomes famous." I took a pause, not really for effect but because I didn't know what the heck I was going to say. "I guess I always knew Lisa would be famous," I started, because it was true. "I just never thought it would happen overnight. I thought I'd have time to prepare, but I got caught totally flat-footed. I haven't written one single chapter of my tell-all memoir."

I got some laughs, especially from the neighbors. "The worst part," I went on, "is that I'm in the video, but nobody knows it, because I'm wearing an egg costume. For the rest of my life, I'm going to be that guy claiming he did something, but he can't prove it, and nobody believes him. Like all those old hippies claiming they were at Woodstock, showing you a photo with four thousand naked people writhing around in the mud and saying 'Look, I swear, that's my butt.'"

MONIQUE BIGBY-HINDS

FAMED BUTT HISTORIAN

"I do not underztand vhy he ees talkink about hees butt!" Klaus whispered to Azure, so loudly that the whole club heard it. He got a bigger laugh than I did.

"And now," I said when it died down, "I have a special treat for you all. I'd like to introduce a man who is one of my personal heroes. A man who has forgotten more about comedy than I'll ever know. Unfortunately, I'm pretty sure he also forgot to shower today."

I heard a loud chuckle to my left and saw Maury Kovalski shuffling toward me. I guess he'd decided that was enough of an introduction.

"Okay, okay, I'll take it from here, sonny boy," he said, shooing me away. I handed him the mic and stepped down into the audience to watch. Maury had said no the first three times I'd asked him to perform, but I knew he was just being difficult. You didn't go around telling that story about Henny Youngman and the pigeon like it was the key to life itself, and then turn down a chance to get onstage.

"Hello there," Maury began, giving the crowd a little wave. "Boy, oh boy. It's been about thirty years since I've stood on a stage like this. And by a stage like this, I mean a stage that might collapse at any minute and kill me. Would it hurt them to spruce this joint up a little bit? I swear, backstage they got an ashtray with half a cigar smooshed in it that Sammy Davis Jr. left there in 1971."

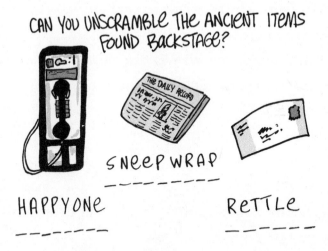

CAN YOU UNSCRAMBLE THE ANCIENT ITEMS
FOUND BACKSTAGE?

SNeePWRAP

HAPPYONe

ReTTLe

He paused and cocked an eyebrow at my friends in the front row. "What am I talking about Sammy Davis for? When were you born? Thursday? Wednesday? I'm surprised you can even dress yourself. I've got cartons of Chinese takeout in my fridge older than you." He threw his hands up. "That's what I get for getting old. Nobody knows what the heck I'm talking about anymore. But the nice thing is, when you're old you can get away with anything. I can go to the grocery store in a bathrobe and bunny slippers, and nobody says a word. They think I'm senile! It's great! Sometimes I walk up to people on the street and ask them for directions to *their* houses, just to see what they say. Sometimes I take my cane and put it right on top of their shoe, and press down as hard as I can, and watch their faces contort in pain—but they don't say anything! They don't want to be rude to an old fart like me!"

By this point, we were all laughing so hard we were crying. But Maury was just getting warmed up.

"I wasn't always this old, you know. I used to be younger. Just yesterday I was younger, as a matter of fact. And believe it or not, I used to be really young! To give you an idea, when I got started in comedy, my first bit was an impression of Abraham Lincoln. The problem was, at that point in time Abraham Lincoln was just a goofy-looking kid a couple years behind me in grade school."

Just then, I heard a noise behind me that I would have recognized anywhere. It sounded like a hyena barfing up three dozen medium-sized Lego pieces, but really it was the way Evan Joseph Healey laughed when he thought something was really, really funny.

I turned and there he was, with tears streaming down his face.

"You came!" I said. Which was pretty much in the category of Extremely Obvious.

"I came," he said, wiping the tears away.

"I was a jerk," I said, and offered him a hand.

"Yup," he said, looking down at my hand as if it was a mackerel or something. "I'm not gonna shake your hand, dude."

"I understand," I said sadly, and dropped it to my side. "I . . ."

"I'm gonna give you a hug, you big dummy."

"Oh!" I said, not sadly. The opposite of sadly, in fact.

He hugged me. It wasn't something we usually did,

me and Evan. But it felt good. I hugged him back and felt a tightness in my chest fade away that I hadn't even realized was there. For the first time in a long time, I was at ease. Like all the wrongs had been righted, and everything was a-okay in the world.

But that wasn't entirely true. There was still one major wrong to right, and it was up to me to make it happen. I told Evan I had some business to take care of, and walked back toward the stage.

CHAPTER 12

Maury was still going strong when I climbed onto the side of the stage, and it took him a few moments to notice me. When he did, he ignored me and kept on telling jokes. That wasn't surprising. I would have done the same thing if some bozo walked onstage during my set.

"So I say to him, 'How much land you got here anyway, mister?' And he says, 'I'll put it like this: if I get in my car and start driving around my property at eight in the morning, I won't get back until eight at night.' 'And so I say, yeah, I used to have a car like that myself.'"

The audience erupted, and Maury covered the microphone with his hand and hissed at me, "Get outta here, kid. Whaddaya trying to do?"

Now everybody else had noticed me onstage, too. I waved my arms for their attention. Maury waved his hands at me to stop. We looked like a pair of crazy cheerleaders.

"Ladies and gentlemen," I said, "I have one more big surprise, seeing as it's Friend Appreciation Night." I turned to Maury. "This one is for you, Mr. Kovalski."

"Don't tell me—you're gonna pay me for my time," he said, and the crowd chuckled.

"Even better," I said. I lifted my eyes to the back of the room and made a beckoning motion.

At my cue, a very large man stood up and began walking toward the stage.

Maury had no idea what was going on. I decided to help him out.

"All the way from South Florida," I said, "may I present . . . Little Abie Mendelson!"

Little Abie walked onstage and took a bow.

"Hiya, Maury," he said. "Long time, eh?"

For a second, I thought Maury was going to keel over. Then he said, "I'm sorry, my hearing's not so good these days. You *are* Little Abie Mendelson? Or you *ate* Little Abie Mendelson?"

Little Abie didn't miss a beat. He folded his arms behind his back, rocked back and forth on his heels, and spoke in a loud, clear voice:

The Spaceman: Ladies and gentlemen, today is a day that shall be remembered throughout the history of mankind. For today, we have reached the planet Mars—and even more astonishing, we have found sophisticated life! I am only a humble spaceman, ladies and gentlemen, but it is my honor to bring you the first interview ever with a real, live Martian!

From the back of the room, Mr. Allen was applauding madly. So were my parents and our neighbors. Suddenly, it hit me that they knew this routine. They had grown up on Maury and Little Abie.

For a few moments, nothing happened. And then I saw a tear streak down Maury's cheek. He wiped it away so fast that I was probably the only one to see it. Me and Little Abie Mendelson,

I mean. The two of them exchanged a look, and I knew something had been communicated between them. Apology, forgiveness, *good to see you, I can't believe how long it's been, boy are you fat, ah shove it.* Something.

And then, just like that, the look was over. Because these guys were professionals, and there was a show to do.

The Spaceman: How are you, sir?

The Martian: Eh, I'm okay, I guess. I just ran out of strudel, which is kind of a bummer. Who are you again? Agnes's nephew?

The Spaceman: No, sir—I am an earthling. A visitor to your planet. Do you mean to say, sir, that you have *strudel* here on Mars?

The Martian: Well, not anymore. We just ran out. Why, did you bring some? *(turns and shouts behind him)* Mabel, there's a strudel delivery guy here!

The Spaceman: No, no, sir—I am from Earth! I've traveled many million miles, and I have to tell you, I'm astounded to find life here on Mars!

The Martian (shrugging): If you call this life.

The Spaceman: What is your name, sir?

The Martian: My name is Zygbabagadoogagadaklooblazoo.

The Spaceman: Z-Zygbabagadoogagadaklooblazoo?

The Martian: Yes, that's right.

The Spaceman: And do you have a last name?

The Martian: Sure. Rothstein.

The Spaceman: Rothstein?

The Martian: Yeah, Rothstein. I know it's a little hard to say.

The Spaceman: And how old are you, Mr. Rothstein?

The Martian: Please, call me Zygbabagadoogagadaklooblazoo. I'm ten minutes old. See, here on Mars, the average life span is only about twenty minutes.

The Spaceman: That must be very stressful, sir.

The Martian: Well, it certainly makes it hard to go to the movies.

The Spaceman: So you're telling me that in only twenty minutes, you are born, you grow up, have children, raise a family—

The Martian: It could be twenty-five, if you're lucky.

My cousin Herman lived to twenty-eight. Boy, was he something. Managed to eat breakfast, lunch, and dinner.

The Spaceman: I must ask you, Mr. Rothstein—

The Martian: Look, no offense, but I feel like I've been talking to you half my life already. My wife probably gave birth to the triplets while we were standing here yapping. They're probably in kindergarten by now.

The Spaceman: Of course, Mr. Rothstein.

The Martian: Unless maybe you have some strudel?

The Spaceman: I think I have one strudel in my space-
ship.

The Martian (clapping him on the back): Now you're
talking!

And they both bowed.
The audience went NUTS.

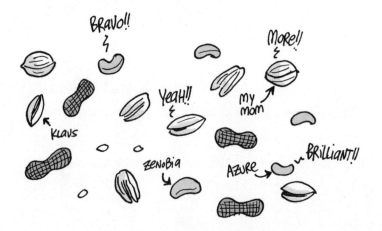

By the time Conceptual Art Band took the stage, everyone was giddy—not just with anticipation but with joy. I didn't find out until I stepped offstage, with Maury's arm around my shoulders and his other arm around Little Abie's. Seeing the two old partners reuniting onstage had been super emotional for everyone. There hadn't been a dry eye in the building, and not just because people laughed until they cried. Although they did that, too.

We made our way to the back of the room as Lisa and Pierre set up. My mom and dad met us there, and soon my whole class was crowding around us. And Evan, who was like an honorary M&AA kid by now.

"I'm proud of you," my dad said.

"You should be," Mr. Allen told him.

"Shhh," Azure said. "Conceptual Art Band is about to start playing."

"They're my favorite band," said Maury Kovalski.

"You and me both," Little Abie Mendelson agreed. "Those kids got moxie!"

"Zey are zuper weird," announced Klaus, then added, "But in a gut way."

"Hey!" Lisa called from the stage.

"Hey!" everybody shouted back.

"We wrote a new song, just for the occasion," she said. "It's called 'The Schlemiel and the Schlimazel: An Ode to Friendship.' Do you guys wanna hear it?"

"Yeah!" everybody yelled, and C.A.B. started playing a fast, peppy tune and singing:

The schlemiel spills the soup.
It lands on the schlimazel.
Friendship isn't easy.
No es fácil.
The schlimazel isn't hostile.
He says to the schlemiel,
The soup was just an appetizer.
Friendship is a meal.
The schlemiel gets a napkin
And wipes his buddy off.
Then they go play golf
And eat some stroganoff, HEY!

I think it's going to be a hit.

No need for a 7-iron in Putt-Putt!!

ABOUT THE AUTHORS

Craig Robinson is an actor, comedian, and musician best known for his work in such films as *Hot Tub Time Machine, Morris from America, This Is the End, An Evening with Beverly Luff Linn,* and *Pineapple Express,* for his role on NBC's *The Office,* and as Leroy in Fox's paranormal comedy series *Ghosted.* But he has not let the fame go to his head like Jake. When he's not filming, Craig might be playing the keyboards with his band Craig Robinson and the Nasty Delicious. Craig lives in Los Angeles and performs worldwide as a stand-up comedian just like Jake (sort of). Discover him on Twitter at @MrCraigRobinson.

Adam Mansbach would never let fame go to *his* head, even though he is the #1 *New York Times* bestselling author of a picture book *about* kids but really for adults. This well-known work—whose title cannot be named here—has been translated into over forty languages and named *Time* magazine's "Thing of the Year." Adam's other novels

have garnered such acclaim as the California Book Award and are taught in hundreds of colleges and universities across the country. He has also written a middle-grade novel about a boy who trades letters with Benjamin Franklin through time, and the screenplay for *Barry*, a biopic about Barack Obama's life as a college student. His work has appeared in the *New Yorker*, the *New York Times*, and *Esquire*, and on NPR's *All Things Considered*. Adam lives in Berkeley, California, and has two daughters whose jokes could compete with Jake's. Find Adam on Twitter at @adammansbach.

ABOUT THE ILLUSTRATOR

Keith Knight, winner of the Glyph, Harvey, and Inkpot Awards, is a spectacular cartoonist whose *Knight Life* comic strip is read nationwide in such newspapers as the *Washington Post*. Keef's funny yet hard-hitting cartoons in his web-comic series *(T)hink* and *The K Chronicles* led him to be named an NAACP History Maker. He is the father of two boys, Jasper and Julian. Catch Keith on Twitter at @KeefKnight.

JAKE THE FAKE PRESENTS:
THE GREATEST FAKES IN HISTORY
(100% REAL!)

GREATEST FAKE SHARK

"Bruce" from the 1975 movie JAWS...

Some say my acting is robotic!

Bruce, the mechanical shark, broke down so often that movie director Steven Spielberg kept the shark from view for most of the film... making it 10,000% scarier!!

GREATEST FAKE GIFT: THE TROJAN HORSE

Yo!! Did someone order online?

The TROJAN HORSE was a WOODEN STATUE given to the city of TROY!! It was STUFFED with GREEK OLIVES!!

Psst!! Troops!! Not olives!!

TROOPS!! (Sorry!! I'm getting hungry!!)

GREATEST FAKE LEGEND:

BIG-FOOT!!

Bigfoot is a large, apelike creature said to inhabit forests, mainly in the Pacific Northwest!! Not to be confused with Chewbacca the Wookiee, who is TOTALLY REAL!!